I0450837

Taken by Three Prison Guards

Taken, Volume 23

Jasmine Black

Published by Spunky Girl Publishing, 2023.

Also by Jasmine Black

Menage
Taken by Three Bikers
Taken by Three Billionaires
Taken by Three Doctors
Taken by Three Cowboys

Menage Series
Taken by Three Bodyguards

Taken
Taken by Two Doctors
Taken by Two Bosses
Taken by Two Firefighters
Taken by Two Personal Trainers
Taken by Two Carpenters
Taken by Two Santas
Taken by Two Lifeguards
Taken by Two Mountain Men
Taken by Two Cops
Taken by Two Prison Guards

Taken by Two Sugar Daddies
Taken by Two X-Husbands
Taken by Three Prison Guards
Taken by Two Elves

The Pleasure Collection
Pleasured by Her Guards
Shared

Standalone
Shared Boxed Set

Taken by Three Prison Guards

Taken Series

Jasmine Black

Twenty-four-years old and eight months pregnant, Madeline "Mad" Madison has been recaptured and sent back to the same prison where she enjoyed being pleasured by two prison guards. It isn't long before the same two men plus a third guard take a naughty interest in her baby blossoming body.

It looks like another escape attempt will just have to wait until Mad's naughty fantasy of being taken by three prison guards becomes a sizzling reality.

(Sequel to Taken by Two Prison Guards)

Other stories by Jasmine Black include:

Taken by Two Doctors, Taken by Three Doctors, Taken by Two Bikers, Taken by Three Bikers, Taken by Two Billionaires, Taken by Three Billionaires, Taken by Two Bosses, Taken by Two Cowboys, Taken by Three Cowboys, Taken by Two Firefighters, Taken by Two Carpenters, Taken by Two Personal Trainers, Taken by Two Santas, Taken by Two Elves, Taken by Three Bodyguards, Taken by Two Cops, Taken by Two Prison Guards, Taken by Two Lifeguards, Taken by Two Mountain Men and more!

License Notes

This book is licensed for your personal use only.

Author Note

This is a work of fiction. Characters, places, settings, and events presented in this book are purely of the author's imagination and bear no resemblance to any actual person, living or dead or to any actual events, places, and/or settings.

Copyright

Chapter One

"Hey, Queen. Nice to see you back. Looks like we can pick right up where we left off."

I trembled with excitement at the familiar nickname and turned toward the voice of Dixon as he and two other prison guards flanked the south side of my cage on the prison exercise yard. I stopped dribbling my basketball inside the twenty-foot by twenty-foot enclosure complete with asphalt ground, a basketball hoop and plenty of metal chain-link fence surrounding me.

I got one hour a day outside in the fresh air and since I was in solitary no one else was around and Dixon could say whatever he wanted if he kept his voice low enough that the security cameras didn't pick up what he was saying.

Dixon had given me plenty of pleasure before I'd escaped. He'd also impregnated me. I suspected on purpose, but hey, maybe the condom ripping had been an accident, like he'd said. But hard to believe, especially since he *did* have a pregnancy fetish.

"And it looks like the Queen has brought along a little present."

Ashton, the other prison guard who'd given me much pleasure right along with Dixon, before I'd left, was staring at my very pregnant belly.

I sighed with resignation as I tossed the ball away. It bounced a few times, rolled against the fence, and stopped.

I'd hoped I'd give birth outside these prison walls, but my luck ran out when someone must have recognized me at one of the places I did housecleaning in a city I'd never expected anyone would know me.

The thought that my sister, Donna, and her husband, might have ratted me out had crossed my mind. They were the only people who knew where I was staying. We'd reconnected after my escape. She'd been thrilled to hear from me, but pissed when I'd told her I'd escaped. She'd gotten all happy when I told her I was pregnant and that I wanted the kid to be born outside of the prison system.

To my surprise she'd helped me get situated in a city about two hours from where she lived and even came to visit. She'd insisted she was careful when driving to my place, reassuring me nobody followed her. We'd had several visits together at my little apartment since I'd settled. She'd even brought my three cute little nieces, all under the age of six. It had been such fun. Life had seemed so normal.

I'd also managed to extract a promise from her that if I'd ever get caught again, she'd take the baby and raise her until I got out. She loved kids, so maybe she *had* screwed me over so she could get my baby all for herself.

Or maybe it had all just been bum luck that someone had seen me and called the cops.

"Just in time for the spring planting too. Not sure how she's going to bend over and plant seeds with that big, voluptuous belly of hers in the way," came a third prison guard's deep guttural voice.

I swallowed and inhaled slowly, calming the anticipation racing through me as I gazed at him. I had never seen him before.

He was cute. Kind of appeared like the accountant type with his dark rimmed glasses, but the rest of him looked strong and muscular, just like Dixon and Ashton.

He wore the traditional guard uniform, just like the other two men. Neatly pressed dark blue shirt, tan pants which was tented quite boldly between his thighs, shiny black boots and a baseball type cap with the words prison guard inscribed in white across the front.

As I studied all the weapons each man wore; guns, batons, tasers, and radios, I pondered how lucky I'd been to escape the prison system.

I grinned inwardly.

Heck, I knew why. These guards thought with their cocks. It was their weakness. I knew what they wanted this time around too. It was in the predatory way they studied me. And in the naughty way my body was humming up a storm of anticipation. Oh, yes, I was going to enjoy picking up where we'd left off.

Only this time I sensed it was going to be three prison guards taking me and not just two. The idea of being in a foursome just about blew my mind and in a really good way.

I'd been in solitary for a couple of weeks since being recaptured and brought back here. But my second night back, I'd discovered the arrangement of butt plugs smuggled in with my supper tray, just like the last time I'd been incarcerated.

The arrival of the plugs had happened mere hours after I'd been intimately examined by the male prison doctor, who, while I'd had my feet in the stirrups, his finger leisurely stroking my clit, had brought me quickly to the edge of climax, while he'd casually commented that it was safe for me to have sexual intercourse right up until the baby came. The baby was still situated quite high inside me, he'd said.

I'd thought he'd meant he'd wanted sex with me, and I would have willingly obliged since he'd aroused me so much, but the examination had ended shortly after, leaving me all hot and bothered.

That same night the butt plugs had appeared.

That's when I knew that Dixon and Ashton wanted me again.

Man, this prison sure did have some naughty stuff going on behind the scenes between the male guards and the female prisoners. All of it illegal of course.

But hey, a girl on the inside had to look out for herself, right? If I had the opportunity for less physical work on the so-called one-woman chain gang, which it appeared was going to be just me again, in trade for some sexual fun, I was all for it.

I would gladly entertain Dixon, with his fetish for pregnant women, and Ashton with the ass fetish.

But what about this new prison guard? What was his thing? I was curious to find out.

"We'll see you bright and early in the morning, baby mama. Make sure your plug is out," Dixon said with a wink.

My pussy creamed up a storm and my ass clenched around the butt plug as I watched all three of them casually walk away.

Oh boy, I could hardly wait until tomorrow.

But in the hot and bothered way I was reacting at the thought of a foursome; I knew I'd need to put out the fire ravaging my aroused body at lights out.

Tonight.

I SCRAMBLED INTO BED and covered myself with the meager blanket supplied by the prison as the lights dimmed signalling time for bed in my solitary cell. I'd spent the afternoon reading, playing solitaire on the laptop, eating supper, talking to my unborn baby, and then doing some light stretches as I tried to distract my mind from fantasizing about having sex with three men.

But every little while the thoughts would turn right back to Dixon, Ashton and that other guard who'd visited me in the yard today.

My thoughts twisted through all kinds of scenarios. Doing oral on them, them taking me anally, vaginally, or both. I'd been thinking up ways where I could just relax and enjoy the outdoor sex while the men did all the work out on the fields.

I chuckled to myself, closed my eyes, and waited for the guard to do his usual check. The guard that I had here in solitary on night duty was an old coot. He looked like a dirty old man, in the way that he leered at me, but he'd always been nice to me.

He was the one who'd brought my supper tray with the butt plugs a couple of weeks back, so it appeared he was in on the shenanigans going on in this prison system too.

I tensed as I heard footsteps approach my cell door. I closed my eyes pretending I was asleep. I heard what I call the Peeping Tom window in the door slide open. The window was what the guards used to look into the cells and take a head count of the prisoners.

I waited and waited. Wondered why he wasn't sliding that window closed quickly like he always did. I mean it only took brief moments to check to see if I was here and hadn't escaped.

A naughty excitement whipped through me. Was he maybe watching me?

I opened my eyes and looked over. No one was there. But the Peeping Tom window was open.

He *had* to be there. I hadn't heard any footsteps leave.

Oh crap. Was he waiting to see if I was up to something? How in the world was I going to pleasure myself if anyone who passed by could look in? Or maybe he was wanting to watch me masturbate?

I sighed as I waited.

"I want to watch you touch yourself," came a man's thick voice.

It was a familiar voice.

It wasn't the old coot. It was that other guard who'd been with Dixon and Ashton earlier today. The one who looked like an accountant with his glasses.

"What's in it for me?" I called out making sure to keep my voice low, despite the fact that knowing he was here for something, was doing some naughty things to my pussy and my ass.

"This," he whispered.

I watched as a small box of chocolates appeared at the window. He let it drop inside.

"Heard you like to get paid up front," he said.

"You heard right," I answered.

Wow, Dixon, and Ashton had given this guard the scoop about me. That I liked to barter my sexual favors to them for something in return.

I dropped my gaze to the box on the floor. Have mercy, those chocolates looked like they were the expensive kind that I'd always wanted to try but couldn't afford.

His face appeared at the Peeping Tom window. He wore his glasses and because lighting in this cell was never completely turned off, I could clearly see from the glittering in his eyes and his wide smile that he was genuinely excited.

"Okay," I breathed as my pussy began to feel hot and heavy.

Just knowing I would have an audience suddenly sent fissures of wicked delight shooting through me.

Man, these pregnancy hormones surely were wreaking impressive new fetishes in me. I'd never really gotten off on someone watching me masturbate, until now.

I sat up, swung my legs over the side of the bed and let the blanket fall off my body, revealing to him my engorged breasts and my swollen abdomen.

I heard his sharp intake of breath. Felt myself respond. My breasts suddenly grew heavier, and my pussy felt weighty and wet.

Chapter Two

I wasn't wearing my nightie as I'd prepared to do some masturbating beneath the blanket, but with him watching, I might as well give him a nice little show, because in behind prison walls, a box of chocolates like the one he'd just dropped into my cell, could cost you a fortune. And if I gave him a good show, he might bring more the next time around.

"So? Are you into pregnant ladies?" I asked, feeling quite comfortable with my nudity.

Over the months, I'd looked at my changing body in the mirror as much as possible. I'd liked what I was seeing. Loved my big belly and big boobies. Had enjoyed how men stared at me. Their eyes watching my every move as I'd gone grocery shopping or cleaned their homes, while their wives were away.

I smoothed my hands over my enlarged breasts. Since my sixteenth week, my breasts had almost doubled in size, and I loved touching them. Tonight, was no different.

"I am into naked pregnant ladies," he admitted.

"Any particular fetish?" I asked.

"Breast feeding, among other things," he whispered in a hoarse voice.

"Oh," I whispered back.

I decided not to ask him about what other things he was into because just touching my breasts was making my breaths come faster and faster and I needed to focus on controlling myself.

"Pull on your nipples, like I'm in there with you, sucking on them," he ordered.

I swallowed at his words. My pussy was already so hot and wet, I wasn't sure if I should touch my nipples, because I just might orgasm. But then again, that was the projected end result now wasn't it.

"Do it, now, please," he said with a groan.

Wow, he really sounded aroused.

"Okay," I replied.

I lifted my hands to my nipples and began twisting them between my forefingers and thumbs.

I gasped as pleasure and pain shot through my sensitive buds, lashed my breasts, and then arrowed down between my thighs like a heat-seeking missile. My ass clenched around the biggest sized butt plug that I'd inserted just before bedtime and my vagina quivered with arousal.

I opened my legs to him, letting him see my pussy. The movement of my ass upon my bed made the plug move deeper and I could feel the entire length of it pushing against my tender anal muscles. It felt just like a cock buried inside me.

I blew out a tense breath as I began plucking my engorged nipples, trying to ignore the wetness that was oozing from them.

"I can see your arousal glistening. At your nipples and at your pussy. Oh, Mad, you're killing me here," he growled.

Man, I was killing myself.

Having someone watching me touching myself was quite the turn on. The air in the cell began to feel hot and so was I as I kept pulling my nipples and then massaging my swollen mounds.

I fought to breathe as I then cupped my full breasts holding them out to him like an offering.

"I'm going to enjoy taking you when the time comes," he muttered from the other side of the Peeping Tom window.

I was looking forward to it too, but I remained quiet, not wanting to break the magnetic mood.

"Now keep touching yourself with one hand and bring your other hand to between your thighs," he instructed in a strangled voice.

Slowly I did as he asked, massaging my left breast while I smoothed my right hand around to cradle my swollen belly then slid lower to between my thighs.

"That's it, now start rubbing that engorged clitoris of yours," he whispered.

I didn't even have to dip a finger into my vagina to get some of my wetness to use for lube as my inner thighs were already drenched with my cream. I smoothed some of the moisture over my middle finger and swept back to do a slow, soft rubbing on my clit. Instantly I felt my body tighten with awareness. My breaths quickened and I closed my eyes as I massaged.

"Harder," he hissed.

I whimpered at his harsh order and collected more of my juices, which felt so slick and thick as I kneaded my tender bundle of nerves. I created a breathtaking friction with my rubbing and everything between my legs quickly went ultra-hot and heavy. My anal muscles tightened, and my aching vagina clenched around emptiness.

I began moaning as nerve endings sparkled with arousal, making me thrust my hips outward, which in turn made my big belly protrude even more. Automatically I spread my legs wider, hoping to cool down the heat a little. But everything was just on fire.

"Now begin pistoning your fingers into your vagina. I want to pretend it's me thrusting my cock into you."

He said the words in such a tortured voice, that I was quite sure he was touching himself on the other side of the door as he viewed me.

I could just imagine him with his pants down, his hands stroking his thick erection as he watched me masturbating.

I could hear his breathing, loud and fast as he watched me slide two fingers into my soaked vagina. I gasped at the pleasure I created as I began to thrust.

"Man, you are so beautiful," he groaned.

I kind of liked that he thought that I was beautiful, but I also knew it was just being said in the heat of the moment.

My fingers slid out of my wet pussy, and I massaged my engorged clitoris until I was moaning from the pleasure. A fiery need for an orgasm quickly spun through me. My body began to ache for release, but I refrained myself. I slowed my thrusts, but I could feel the pulse of arousal continue to build.

I arched my hips some more, pressing my feet into the hard cement floor.

The guard was groaning, and I sensed he was nearing his climax, so I figured it was time to join him.

I increased the depth of the thrusts, went faster and faster, plunging my fingers deeper and deeper, until my thighs were so tight, they ached. Then suddenly I was convulsing, my body shuddering uncontrollably as the waves of pleasure ripped through me like a wild storm.

I gasped at the intensity.

Cried out as I bucked my hips and plunged my fingers harder into my pussy, bringing more pleasure waves.

I was shaking as if being electrified, my legs and lower belly trembling. My vagina clenched like a vice around my fingers and every time I withdrew there came a wet sucking, popping sound that split through the air. The sound joined the guard's guttural groans and my excited cries as the orgasm continued pounding me with pleasure and then all too soon, the magnificent spasms ebbed away.

I lay back down on the bed, gasping and spent, wishing he'd come into my cell and bring me to another orgasm himself.

But he didn't.

Instead, all I heard was the rustle of clothing and I envisioned he was pulling up his pants and putting on his weapons.

"See you tomorrow, Queen," he whispered.

Then the Peeping Tom window slid closed.

I smiled. Tomorrow couldn't come soon enough.

It was time to indulge in an after-sex treat. Slowly, I got out of the bed and headed for the box of chocolates.

THE NEXT MORNING CAME really fast, and my head was spinning as I was led in wrist restraints along the various narrow, concrete hallways, by an incredibly quiet guard from solitary. We stopped every now and again in front of a locked metal door where the guard talked on his radio instructing someone to buzz us through. Finally, he unshackled my wrist restraints and then left me in the room where they kept the work gear for the prisoners of the chain gangs.

I was stunned when I entered the room and found five other female inmates picking out their gear. They were all obviously pregnant, in various stages.

I was the one furthest along. The biggest.

When they saw me, they all stared.

"Wowser. Look at what the tomcats dragged in," one of the prison inmates finally cackled.

She appeared to be the oldest of them. Her face was wrinkled, her eyes squinting with plain anger. Her black hair was pulled back in a severe bun and her mouth was set in a spiteful, bitter way as she caressed her protruding belly while she studied me when I stood just inside the doorway.

"Yum yum another one with a bun in the oven. I wonder which detail she'll get," another inmate cawed. She looked to be in her forties and her blonde hair was cut short to her scalp. Her dark gaze looked me up and down like I was trash.

I bristled, pushing down the urge to spit in her face.

"She's for the guards with the pregnancy fetish, of course. Good thing she came back, now we'll get a reprieve from all that sex those guards are dishing out," yet another woman, with tattoos all over her face, said.

All the women laughed. Irritation snapped within me. but I held my temper.

I didn't recognize any of them from my earlier incarceration, which meant rumors were already flying that I was back in custody.

"Sex? I don't know what you're yapping about. I'm on planting detail," I replied coolly.

The walls had ears. I wasn't about to give them any information on any of the guards. These comments from the prisoners could be a test by the guards themselves to see how much I would talk. But then again, why would they put out feelers? I could have blown the whistle on their set up anytime over the course of the last eight months after escaping. But I didn't. I'd kept a low profile, yet here I was again.

"Leave her alone. She ain't talking," yet another inmate said.

She looked to be the youngest of the group. Probably around my age and her baby belly was almost as big as mine. She was pretty with wavy shoulder length auburn hair and bright blue eyes. She had a cute Marilyn Monroe type dark mole halfway between her upper left lip and cheek.

To my surprise, she reached out her hand in introduction.

"I'm Jenny," she said.

Seriously? She *had* to be a newbie.

I mean, who introduced themselves with a handshake in prison? I'd certainly not come across a handshake in my years on the inside.

Compassion for her bombarded me. She seemed innocent and vulnerable but there was also an edge of something dark that she must have gone through. I could read it in her eyes.

Reluctantly, I reached out and shook hands with her. Her fingers warmly wrapped around mine and for some crazy reason, I felt as if I'd just made a friend.

"Mad, short for Madeline," I replied.

"What are you in for?" she asked as she let go of my hand.

"Murder."

Her eyes widened at my response, and she said nothing. She kind of looked surprised. Don't know why because lots of women were in here for murder.

Oh well, so much for making a friend. When she said nothing more, I decided to move on.

I strolled to the area at the back of the room where a bunch of used work boots were neatly lined on several shelves.

"I'm in for attempted murder," she suddenly said from right behind me.

I nodded, picked out a pair of well-worn boots that looked my size, then sat down on a bolted metal chair to try them on. They fit surprisingly well. I kept the boots on, figuring I'd walk around a bit to make sure they were okay.

"Yeah, she tried to kill her husband after he decided he didn't want another baby," the oldest inmate with the wrinkled face yapped in a snide tone as I tossed my prison issue running shoes along the wall where the others had left their shoes.

"Keep your mouth shut concerning other people's business," I snapped at the bitch, suddenly feeling protective of Jenny.

"Or what? You wanna beat me and my baby up?" The old bag prattled, her bushy eyebrows arching in defiance as she patted her rounded belly.

"Yeah, you'd probably be beating up your baby's sibling," the inmate with the tattoos snickered.

Oh, lovely. Had Dixon gotten all these women pregnant just so he could titillate his pregnancy fetish?

I should be pissed off, but I wasn't. It was survival mode in prison, and we all did what we had to do to survive and keep as comfortable as possible.

"Oh, don't listen to them, Mad. They're just jealous. We've all been knocked down the totem pole so-to-speak with you being back. Word has it, you're Dixon and Ashton's favorite," Jenny replied in a muffled voice that was meant for only me to hear.

I merely nodded, and hurried over to find a jumpsuit that would fit me. I should be pleased that Dixon and Ashton favored me, but I didn't like the idea that these women knew that kind of information.

Just then I noticed a guard standing in the doorway. I recognized him as the one who'd come to my Peeping Tom window last night.

He was studying me with a rapt expression. His glasses illuminated the color of his eyes, which were a green that reminded me of the color of leaves when they first unfurled in the Spring.

I trembled as lust spun through me remembering last night's masturbating session with him watching.

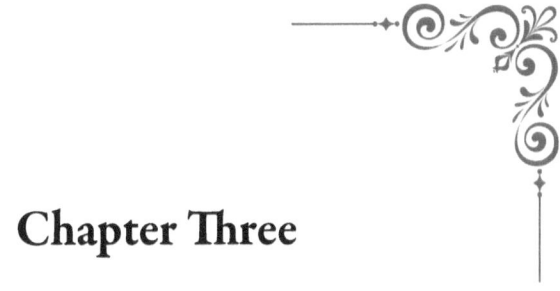

Chapter Three

D ue to my pregnancy, my hormones for sex were in overdrive. I'd read that many women didn't want sex while they were pregnant, but I'd gone the opposite way. Instead of craving pickles drenched in ice cream or wanting greasy French fries covered in yogurt, I craved sex, and I wanted it pretty much all the time.

Outside of the prison walls, I had masturbated like mad, trying to keep myself satisfied. Now, with my being on the inside again, I hoped the guards would alleviate my sexual needs.

"Hurry up, ladies. Your chariots await," the guard called out to all of us.

He held my gaze and winked.

I looked away, quickly heading for the bin with the work gloves.

The wheels were turning in my mind. The last time I was on the so-called one-woman chain gang I'd managed to get Dixon and Ashton to do most of the work. In return, I got fresh air with my naked body bathed in sunshine in the open fields and I gave them my body so they could pleasure me and themselves.

I hoped this guy was just as easy to manipulate.

"Leo seems eager this morning," Jenny chuckled as I picked a pair of well-worn gloves that I hoped I wouldn't be using. Much.

Leo, so that was that guard's name.

Quickly I slipped off the boots, stepped into the pant legs of the jumper and then pulled on the rest of the orange suit, which really illuminated my pregnant belly. I slipped my feet into the boots again and stuffed the work gloves into a jumper pocket.

Then I caught Leo waving me over. Wrist and ankle shackles dangled from his hands.

"You finished, Mad?" he shouted.

I nodded. He looked kind of cute, wearing black rimmed glasses. Kind of smart, too. Hopefully not too smart.

"Jenny Palmer and Mad, you two ladies are coming with me," he called out.

Shit. I sure hoped he was dropping her off somewhere else. How was I supposed to have sex with another chick around?

Jenny gently elbowed me in the ribs.

"Looks like the guys want a little extra special fun today," she whispered.

I frowned, not knowing what she meant.

"The rest of you, wait here. Your chariot is coming," Leo said.

Another guard stood behind Leo and his hand was close to his taser as he warily watched me.

I laughed inwardly.

Seriously? He thought I was going to make an escape attempt inside prison walls?

"Hold out your hands, Mad," Leo commanded in a stern voice.

Irritation snapped through me at the sound of the rattling chains as, while the other guard watched his back, Leo quickly shackled first my wrists and then my ankles. I really didn't like the clinking of the chains. They reminded me that my fate was sealed.

Because I'd escaped, they had tacked another five years onto my sentence. They probably figured the add on would deter me from another escape attempt.

I frowned. If that were the case, they had me pegged wrong.

I watched as he shackled Jenny.

Then he opened the door and waved for Jenny and me to go ahead. I stepped past the other guard who continued staring at me with what I figured was suspicion and hurried along with Jenny close behind.

Moments later, Jenny and I were cuffed to our metal seats at the back of a prison van.

Thankfully, Jenny remained silent as she looked out the window.

I remembered my first time getting outside the prison walls. It had been after five years. I'd been so glad seeing the wide-open sky and the land spreading out as far as I could see without walls blocking my view.

Yeah, getting out of here during the days would make life in prison semi-bearable. That is until I figured out a way to escape again.

The drive was along the same route as I remembered. There were ladies wearing prison orange jumpsuits who picked up garbage and tree branches from the ditches on both sides of the desolate highway, while male guards watched them, their arms crossed leisurely over their chests, or their hands nestled close to their weapons.

At one point I had wanted to work on a chain gang, just so I could be on the outside. But it hadn't worked out that way. Instead, *I had been* the chain gang, but I'd finagled deals with my guards. They worked, I mostly watched, or did the easy stuff and we all had sex.

Now, exactly how was I supposed to do that with an audience of Jenny, that is if she was staying?

I had removed my butt plug this morning as Dixon had instructed yesterday in the yard. My ass was wide open, waiting to be filled by a luscious cock and my pussy was quivering and clenching, wanting a delicious penis thrusting into me.

Damn, I guess that wasn't happening today.

I closed my eyes and moaned softly as disappointment rocked me.

"Don't worry, we're almost there," Jenny whispered.

I opened my eyes and found her staring at me. She was cradling her big baby belly. She smiled at me with what I figured was reassurance.

Huh, she looked cute when she smiled.

I watched as she slowly licked her bottom lip, giving me a glimpse of a gold ball near the tip of her tongue.

Oh dear. She had a piercing on her tongue.

I knew some women had their tongues pierced for their men. It was meant to increase their significant other's oral pleasure. I doubt I would do something like that for a man. Why ruin my tongue? Anyways, to each their own, or however the saying goes.

Nervousness rippled through me as the van turned off the highway onto a narrow dirt road. On both sides of the road, I could see freshly tilled fields of black earth. From the looks of it there was lots of planting to be done which made me wonder exactly how was I going to bend over and plant with my big baby belly in the way?

I held my breath as the van turned yet again onto another road. This one was quite bumpy and very narrow.

The prettiest blue Scotch pine trees lined both sides of the farmer's lane, and I couldn't help but smile as memories of my mom coming home one day before Christmas lugging a most beautiful six-foot-tall blue Scotch pine tree into the house.

It had been the first Christmas after Dad had abandoned us. It had looked just like these trees. She'd paid a lot for that beautiful tree, and it had been worth all the money with its perfect branches that proudly held the homemade ornaments of coloured paper rings and popcorn strands that my sister and I had created. Mom had also made some cute little crocheted Santa hats and knitted black bear ornaments; from skeins of yarn, she'd gotten for free from an elderly lady she cleaned house for.

"There they are," Jenny's excited voice broke into my memories, and I followed her gaze. She was looking past the rusty cage bars that separated the back of the van with the front.

Past the windshield, up ahead, I spied another prison van.

My breaths came faster as I spied Dixon and Ashton standing in front of the van, wearing the traditional dark blue shirts, tan pants and caps. They watched as we approached.

A moment later, Leo stopped the vehicle.

"Alright, ladies. Time to get to work," he called out.

A moment later, the side door suddenly slid open, and Ashton stood there. He was smiling at me, and my pulse quickened as I gazed at him. He was quite handsome and still possessed that same predatory look that I remembered so well. My gaze dropped to between his thighs and my pussy creamed as I noticed his tented pants.

Have mercy, he was already quite aroused.

"Good morning, my Queen. I can see you're all tied up at the moment."

Oh lovely, prison humor.

"Ha, ha, ha," I answered with a fake smile.

That's when something suddenly dawned on me. I don't know why it hadn't occurred to me until right now. Probably because everything had happened so fast that I really hadn't had the time to process fully that I was back in the pen, but now I wondered if Dixon and Ashton might have revenge on their minds. Revenge of what I had done to them in order for me to escape.

I blew out a tense breath as Leo entered the van.

He towered over me as he withdrew a ring of keys from his pant pocket. Then he inserted a key into the handcuff he'd used to secure the chain of my wrist shackles to a metal bar on the seat. I heard a click, and he took the cuffs.

Then he released Jenny.

"Up and out," Leo instructed.

He stood and waited for us to get off our seats. I sensed in the quick way he was breathing that he was aroused too.

My mouth grew dry as I hobbled down the few steps of the van, the rattling chains of my wrist and ankle restraints driving me nuts. Fresh, mild air breathed against me and when my feet hit the ground, I stifled the overpowering need to run and to just be free again.

Jenny followed and we stood in front of the guards awaiting their orders.

Dixon held a clipboard and as he gazed at me, my heart skipped a beat at those gorgeous aqua blue eyes. They were so illuminated when the sun shone on his face. Wow, how had I forgotten about his delicious looking, blue-colored eyes?

"Just want to confirm you are Madeline Madison. In for aggravated manslaughter, fifteen years to life."

That he said fifteen years instead of the usual ten years irked me. Obviously, they knew about that extra five years tapped onto my sentence for my escape. Man, nothing was private around here.

He looked up from his clipboard awaiting my answer. Did I detect the slightest smile on his lips?

I nodded.

He looked at Jenny.

"And you are Jennifer Lynn Palmer. In for attempted murder. Twenty to life."

"Yes, sir," she replied in a firm voice.

Dixon wrote something down on his clipboard and then tossed it into his van. He shut the door and stepped in behind me and Jenny.

Ashton waved at us to follow them along a trail between the Scotch pine trees. On the other side of the trees was a large freshly tilled field of dark earth, a bright blue tractor that had some weird square funnel contraption with shiny silver metal discs attached beneath the funnel.

There was also a bunch of heavy looking bags set near the tractor.

Corn seeds, the bags, said.

"Oh, lovely, we're playing farmers today." Jenny said from beside me.

"That's right. You two are the cows. You'll give us farmers some milk," Dixon replied.

I trembled and almost moaned out loud as I remembered how Dixon and Ashton's mouths had sucked on my nipples during my last incarceration. Man, those men knew how to make a woman feel good.

Now with my being pregnant, my breasts were even more tender, and my nipples engorged.

Chapter Four

"Now, now. Work first," Leo admonished Dixon as he strolled over to inspect the corn bags.

"Okay ladies, your job will be to follow the tractor, making sure all the corn seeds are covered. If you see one that isn't, bend over, and cover it up by hand," Ashton said in a no-nonsense tone of voice.

Shit! Was he for real?

"Oh, and if you ladies want us to help you, you'll have to give us a little incentive," Dixon broke in.

Now, they were talking. I blew out a slow tense breath as anticipation whipped through me. That they were talking so freely in front of Jenny must mean she knew what was going on and that she was part of the party today.

"And what would that be?" I asked, knowing that we had entered the negotiation phase. We do something for the guards. And the guards would help us out.

Ashton and Dixon were staring over at Leo, obviously giving him first choice.

"Bare your breasts while you work," came Leo's quiet response.

My pussy grew hot at his words. And I could hear Jenny inhale sharply.

Whether her response was out of surprise, inexperience, or excitement, I wasn't sure but for some crazy reason, I wanted to see her breasts too.

Jenny began to unzip her jumper, but I grabbed her wrist, stopping her.

Ashton cursed softly.

"Shit, Queen. What is the matter? You should be bending over and letting each of us take turns with you and that's just to start the payback you owe us," Dixon commented angrily.

I trembled with anticipation at his words, but I needed to keep this professional so-to-speak for now.

"My apologies, gentlemen, but if you two were too stupid to fall asleep while on duty, there is no payback. Now how about we get down to business? I want half an hour uninterrupted break times for both Jenny and I, plus a two-hour lunch for us. If you feel that is a good deal for today, then we'll gladly bare our breasts for you to watch, but the men will have to do the bending over to cover up the seeds while we point them out."

I had spoken with such confidence, the three guards were staring at me, their mouths partially open as if catching flies.

Beside me, Jenny didn't say a word either and from the corner of my eye I could tell she had a shocked expression.

"On one condition," Dixon said in a strangled voice.

"And that would be? I asked.

"You and Jenny play with each other's breasts after lunch, while we watch," Dixon said.

"No worries. We'll put on a nice show for you. Deal," I replied.

The three men moved away, and Jenny tugged on my elbow.

"Are you sure about this? I mean, I've never done this with a woman."

Oh, great. She had to be a newbie. This was not what I needed. Hopefully, this would be a one day thing with her along today.

"No worries. We'll discuss everything later."

I knew from past boyfriends, especially from the asshole that I had supposedly murdered, accidentally, of course, that men enjoyed watching two women touching each other among other naughty things. It would get the guards in the mood for sex and cloud their judgement for better deals that I could get.

Hey, there was a method to my madness.

The three guards were laughing as they joyfully began dumping out the contents of the seed bags into that long narrow funnel like contraption on the trailer behind the tractor.

I smiled to myself.

I bet had I not gotten us a sweet deal, the two of us would have been made to dump all those bags, instead of the guards. I remember the warden warning me on my first day back that just because I was pregnant, I would not be getting any special treatment.

But these men pretty much thought with their down south heads, instead the head on their shoulders, so the warden was wrong about the non-existent special treatment.

I unzipped my jumper, slipped my arms out of the sleeves, and tied the sleeves around my waist. Then I lifted my T-shirt. I had gone without a bra today knowing something like this would happen, so my big breasts bounced free. And I got a bit excited as Jenny stared at them.

"Your turn," I instructed as I flung my top over a nearby bush, ignoring the two pinpricks of wetness where leakage from my nipples had stained the top.

Jenny swallowed and unzipped her jumpsuit. She tied the sleeves around her waist in the same way I had done. Then she lifted her prison issue T-shirt and placed it beside my shirt. Her bra wasn't in the best of shape and it did a lousy job supporting her pregnancy boots, but hey, that was prison life. Not the best clothing or undergarments available for the lowly prisoners.

I reined in my momentary self pity party. The system was what it was. Nothing I could do about it, so why think about it.

I watched as Jenny slid down her bra straps and then she turned her back to me.

What? Was she freaking serious? She was shy at me seeing her breasts? In prison?

Oh, my goodness. All the women saw each other naked in here, especially during showers. Or in their shared cells.

"Can you unclasp me?" she asked.

I sighed with relief.

Man, for a minute I thought for sure I had some shy twit on my hands.

"Sure."

I unclasped her bra and it burst loose like an explosion.

Geez. Talk about tight.

I found myself going wide-eyed as she turned around and let the bra drop away.

Wow. Her breasts were bigger than mine. And her nipples were huge. The prison guards were going to have a field day with the two of us.

But hey, as long as they did most of the work, then Jenny and I could be the ornaments, instead of the other way around.

I noticed the prison guards had stopped talking. I looked over and saw them watching us. Some naughty thrills zipped through me at their scorching looks.

Yeah, if looks good fuck, they would be doing us right now.

"Okay, showtime," I murmured to Jenny.

"I do like the way they are looking at us," she said with a giggle.

"You'll get used to it," I lied.

I swear it looked like their eyes were going to pop out of their sockets as we walked toward them topless, our full breasts bouncing with each step.

I heard Dixon, the father of my baby, curse softly.

"Only looking. No touching. Let's get to work, gentlemen. Play time is later," I said.

I smiled inwardly as the three men moved like a well-oiled unit to my instruction.

"You would think you're the boss," Jenny whispered.

"We have the power of females over them. You just gotta learn how to utilize it. Especially in a prison with male guards," I commented in a low voice, so they didn't hear.

She didn't say anything, but with the smile on her face. I could almost hear the wheels grinding in her brain.

Maybe a new queen was being born?

Jenny and I walked behind the tractor and the seeding machine pointing out areas that hadn't been covered by dirt while the men used shovels to cover them. I could tell the equipment was old and rusty. That's why certain parts didn't work right leaving a trail of seeds here and there and why things on the tractor squeaked and clattered.

I knew that having us here was a cheap form of labor for the farmer, which made me wonder why I had never actually *seen* a farmer during my previous ventures out to the farmland. Unless the land belonged to the prison system, which I highly suspected, especially since the guards allowed Jenny and me to walk bare breasted in the field without seeming worried at getting caught.

Again, who was I to question the setup?

As long as I got some warm sunshine, exercise and I was free of the boring routine of the prison, all was good.

I was impressed with Jenny. She concentrated really hard on her job, and she seemed oblivious to the prison guards leering gazes. Maybe she was pretending she was free too?

Well, break time couldn't come soon enough for me. The chaffing and the clanking of our leg and wrist chains was grinding on my nerves. My baby bump felt ultra heavy, like it was dropping, my kid was kicking up a storm and I needed to go to the bathroom.

Most of all I needed a rest from the hot stares of the guards because their scorching looks were seriously turning me on. I hadn't had sex with a man since I'd escaped this place just under eight months ago.

On the outside I hadn't wanted to risk a relationship. I had come close on a couple of occasions, but I'd been strong and given each interested guy the cold shoulder.

When Dixon called break, my breasts were feeling quite weighty, and my nipples were tender and wet. The gusting of the warm wind against my nipples felt like a man blowing his breath against them, and I kept having visions of two of the guards popping my nipples into their mouth, which in turn made my pussy cream and my ass clench.

During break, we were accompanied by Leo to a nearby outhouse. He kept staring at our breasts with hungry looks, but he kept quiet.

Afterwards, he led us back to where we'd first started earlier this morning. He left us and returned to Ashton who was standing beside the pile of corn seed bags drinking what I assumed was water from a plastic bottle.

Jenny had grabbed her long-sleeved T-shirt off the bush and placed the garment around her neck to let the sleeves dangle, partially covering her breasts. But I could see the voluptuous curve every time she lifted her arm to wipe away the perspiration beading her forehead and the sight was turning me on.

I, however, decided to leave my breasts exposed to the mild sunshine and that naughty wind. It felt good to have my upper half naked. Had I my wish, I would work fully naked. But I wasn't that bold. At least not yet. Thankfully, the baby had settled down as there was no more kicking.

"I'm so thirsty," Jenny complained as she we sat on the cool ground.

Because it was spring, the grass was short and slender, and the leaves were just bursting like little emerald jewels on the nearby bushes. Everything looked so green and new, and it made me feel happy, despite my circumstances.

"They'll bring water soon," I said.

I was pretty thirsty too. And I wished I could pour some cold water over my breasts and cool down those hot nipples.

"Who's thirsty?"

Dixon was suddenly here, bursting from behind the pine trees, and he held a small blue plastic water jug and two large paper cups.

"I am!" Jenny exclaimed.

"It's all yours. Enjoy."

He handed her the water jug and tossed the two paper cups onto the ground in front of my feet.

If he expected a thanks, he wasn't getting it from me. Or from Jenny because she had already grabbed a cup and was hurriedly pouring herself a drink.

Dixon just stood there and gazed down at me. Well, actually he stared at my breasts which made me want him to grab his head and bury his face there. Mentally I shook that naughty thought away.

"Uninterrupted break. That was the deal," I snapped at him.

He nodded and his blue eyes flashed beneath the sunlight, making my breath catch at the impressive aqua color.

"One question. Is that kid really mine?" he asked.

I felt insulted. The son of a bitch sure had nerve.

"Of course, it's yours. Or did Ashton's condom break too?"

He frowned.

"No other guys since us?"

"That's two questions. Not that it is any of your business but no, just you two. Now, fuck off," I replied, irritation simmering through me. I wanted him gone until the time came when I needed him to relieve me.

He nodded.

"Okay, okay. Take it easy. I'm going, but when it comes time to take you, I will be the first to do it," he growled.

"Knock yourself out," I replied cooly.

Tell the truth. I couldn't wait to have sex with him again.

I smiled inwardly and enjoyed the way his lips thinned like he was pissed off at my reply. I thought he might say something, but he didn't. Instead, he walked away and joined Ashton and Leo, who were talking quietly amongst themselves.

"Wow, he allows you to talk to him like that. I'd get solitary for a week if I mouthed off to a guard," Jenny said as she poured some water into the other cup and handed it to me.

"Well, he *is* the father of my kid. I think I have every right to talk to him like that," I blurted.

"Was it co-sensual?" she asked in a faint voice.

I kind of stared at her. I wanted to tell her to mind her own business, but she had this weird look of caring on her face that made me want to tell her the truth.

BESIDES, DIXON HAD been so stupid to ask that question about the kid being his right in front of a third party. What a dumb fuck. Cat was out of the bag now.

But Jenny knowing the truth gave me a sense of safety. Now, he would have to make both of us disappear in order to keep his secret.

"Yeah, the sex was co-sensual, but I believe the broken condom was intentional."

Jenny's eyes widened in surprise.

Chapter Five

"Really? How so?" she asked.

"Previous conversations about him having a thing for pregnant women. You heard him earlier too. He said we were cows, and we would supply milk."

I decided to clam up. I had said too much.

"I swear I won't share what you've just told me," she said, as if knowing exactly what I was thinking.

"You better keep your mouth shut if you know what's good for you. I have a good thing going here as you can see. If I hadn't struck that deal for us, we would be nursing sore backs and calloused palms," I warned.

Jenny bit her bottom lip and nodded.

"I'll keep a close watch on how you operate, so I can learn from you, Teach," she said after a few moments of silence.

"Just don't share with anyone what you learn, or we won't be allowed to leave the prison walls. I just about went nuts on the inside last time. It took me almost five years to get onto a work detail. I was kind of expecting the same long wait this time, but I guess Dixon and Ashton must have pulled strings in order to get me out here again."

She arched an inquiring eyebrow.

"And it doesn't bother you? Having sex with the guards?"

"Why should it? Did you ever go without sex with a man for five years? I need it like people use water," I explained.

Jenny said nothing as she stared off into the distance.

Although it would have been better had this relationship with the baby's father not be kept a secret. I mean, how the hell was I going to explain to my kid how he or she was conceived? That he or she was the result of the broken condom as I was being double penetrated by prison guards. Yeah, I would never tell my kid the truth.

And I needed to shut up. I was treating her like she was my priest, and I was in a confessional booth.

We sat quietly for the rest of the break, each of us in our own worlds as we gazed around at our surroundings of tilled fields and at the black crows and white seagulls that flew around overhead beneath a bright sun that shone brilliantly in a pristine blue sky.

"Back to work, ladies!" Leo called out after awhile.

"Oh, fun," Jenny muttered as she struggled to get up. Her big baby bump prevented her from standing and the guards certainly weren't coming over to help her.

"Hold on, I'll give you a hand," I said as I stood up with relative ease despite my bulk.

While I'd had been on the outside, I'd made it a habit of keeping fit because I'd heard it was better for the baby, so my workouts were paying off out here.

I gave Jenny my hand and she fought to haul herself up.

My gaze dropped to her breasts as she placed her long sleeved T-shirt onto the bush.

Man, her nipples looked like giant ruby red lollipops and for some crazy reason, I couldn't wait to get a taste of them.

Give your head a shake, I chastised myself. She's a woman.

But still, there was something about those ripe curves of hers that did something naughty deep inside my womb. Probably those pregnancy hormones of mine acting up again.

Oh well, it was time to get back to the chore of screwing the puppy.

I grinned as I followed Jenny back to the field.

ASHTON AND DIXON CERTAINLY remembered that I loved proper food. Because at lunch time both Jenny and I were presented with store bought fried chicken, fries, salad, and an ice-cold pop that Dixon must have gotten for us after he'd disappeared for awhile and had returned at the start of lunch.

"Man, this tastes like heaven," I said around a mouthful of juicy chicken.

"Don't it, though," Jenny answered.

Thankfully, the guards were leaving us in peace so I could truly enjoy my meal and not think about smearing chicken juices on their cocks before taking each one of their shafts into my mouth.

Whew! My hormones were really working overtime when those men were staring and they were staring at the two of us as they ate their own food, which appeared to be homemade sandwiches.

I opted to leave my breasts bared, mainly because my nipples felt tender. Covering them would just make them chafe erotically against my clothing. But I did love their hot stares. It turned me on to be appreciated. Too bad the circumstances weren't different, but hey, it was what it was.

Jenny and I ate the rest of our meal in silence. I focused my attention to the crystal-clear blue sky, loving the brilliant color. I soaked in all the scenery like I was a sponge. The freshly seeded black soil, the groundhog that scampered along the far edge of the field. The grey rock boulders that lined the area like a wall. Hell, I preferred a rustic stone wall like that one compared to the cinder blocks and razor wires keeping us captive.

"So, who did you try to murder?" I asked Jenny after I completed my meal.

She had just finished with her macaroni salad, so I figured it was okay to ask. You know in case the question made her lose her appetite.

She didn't say anything. She just kind of got a hard expression that chased away the innocent vulnerable look that I'd liked and then she stared off across the field.

Okay, I guess it wasn't any of my business. I could take a hint.

So, I kept quiet and just shrugged my shoulders, trying to loosen them up from all that walking behind that clattering seeding machine.

Like talk about a real joke of a job.

I mean, I could probably finagle it so I could watch the guards work all day and take turns having sex with them, but not with Jenny around. At least not until I got to know her a bit more, which was kind of silly because I couldn't wait to play with her luscious looking breasts.

"I tried to murder my husband, after he tried to kill our baby," Jenny suddenly said.

I felt my eyes widen in surprise at her admission.

"He was a big man. Very good looking. Very charismatic. You know the kind, the loudest at the party. The one who has so many friends."

I nodded but kept quiet so she could talk.

"I went to a party that friends of a friend were throwing. He was on me pretty fast at the party. He kept chasing after me, chatting me up, telling me he liked the way I looked, loved the way I laughed."

Jenny grimaced and took a sip of her pop and then continued.

"I was so shy back then. I didn't have much confidence. My parents were assholes; verbally and physically abusive toward each other and toward me. So yeah, I liked his attention. Once he figured out, I had no boundaries he encouraged me to move into his place within a couple of weeks. Had me pregnant within a couple of months and married me a month after that. It was a whirlwind. He was so kind, and I thought I'd hit the jackpot. But I ignored all the signs. You know the red flags. His subtle put downs disguised as jokes. He didn't want me talking to men because it made him so jealous.

So, I tried not to make eye contact with men when he was around. He didn't like my folks. Hell, neither did I, so, I stop talking to them.

He didn't like my friends, so I stopped talking to them. He didn't like my job, so I stayed home to serve him. Then when he had me hooked onto him, he became violent. It started with slaps, then came the fists, then I lost the first baby..."

"Fuck," I whispered.

I thought I'd had it bad with my man with all his running around, but Jenny's husband sounded like a real jerk. I protectively placed my hands upon my belly. No way would anyone hurt my baby.

"After I lost the baby, I got into one bad depression. I couldn't eat. I couldn't sleep. I stayed in bed. He liked the stay in bed part."

Jenny patted her belly.

"Every time he sensed I was pregnant he'd punch the crap out of me. I lost three babies before I finally came to my senses. He was a cop, so I helped myself to his revolver one night after he beat the shit out of me, fucked me and fell asleep. Literally, in that order. I took the gun, rested the muzzle against his temple and pulled the trigger. I figured he was dead. There was so much blood. So, I called 911 and I confessed. I figured I'd stick with the self defence story, but hell, he survived. Who would have thought that? He said he was defending himself when I tried to go after him with his gun, that's why I had so many bruises. Well, of course the cop always wins as they always tell the truth, right? He even swore his lies on the bible in court. So here I am."

My head was spinning.

"That's freaking crazy. I am so sorry you had to go through all that," I told her, feeling really bad for her.

Her hand leisurely caressed her baby bump. And she smiled at me.

"You need to appeal," I said.

"It'll all work out. You'll see," she replied.

"Shit, I hope you're not just going on faith, because that don't work in the legal system," I spat.

Man, someone needed to knock some sense into this girl. She just kept smiling, like she suddenly had no care in the world.

"It's not your problem, Mad. Let's just enjoy the sunshine and what's coming after lunch. To tell you the truth, I'm looking forward to putting on a good show for the guards."

I couldn't help but laugh.

"Well, I am glad you're glad. I plan on leaving them with such hard-ons that they can't get rid of them."

It was Jenny's turn to giggle.

Wow, with all the shit she'd gone through she could still laugh. She was an amazing woman.

The rest of our lunch drifted by, and we remained quiet, alone in our thoughts.

Near the end of lunch, we took turns going to the outhouse, which was conveniently located where the guards could keep their eyes on us. We used the rest of the water from the water jug to wash our hands and rinse out our mouth. Then we began plotting on what show we would give to the guards.

"Alright ladies, time is up," Leo called out later and motioned for us to go over to them.

Jenny unzipped her jumpsuit and worked her arms out of the sleeves. She tied her sleeves beneath her breasts, removed her top and bra and displayed her heavy breasts to me. It was cool that she wasn't shy about showing off her assets.

Oh boy, had someone told me just this morning that I would get turned on seeing a woman's milk engorged boobs, I would have decked them.

Jenny was different though. I felt as if I'd found a kindred spirit in her. Like I could really like her.

"Showtime," she said and wiggled her eyebrows and headed toward the guards. Her walk was full of confidence, her shoulders pushed back making her chest quite prominent.

Chapter Six

"Ladies, I hope you had an enjoyable lunch, now let's see what you've got for us," Ashton said in a thick, aroused voice as we joined the three men.

I dropped my gaze to the apex of his thighs. Oh, yes, his pants were tented nicely. And so were Dixon's and Leo's pants.

Man, these guards were so predictable.

"We'll need the restraints off, so we can give you all a nice show," I suggested.

I'd expected an argument, but Leo eagerly moved forward. I watched as he withdrew his ring of keys from his pocket, and within moments Jenny and I were free from our wrist restraints and then to my further surprise he also released the ankle restraints.

Wow had I known it would be this easy to get my way, I would have asked for them off earlier.

Jenny turned toward me, her gaze capturing mine. Her eyes sparkled with eagerness and there was a big, beautiful smile on her face as she began caressing her rounded breasts.

My pussy clenched with arousal, and I turned to face her.

I heard Dixon moan and Ashton and Leo gasp.

I lifted my hands and began teasingly caressing my voluptuous breasts. Everywhere I touched, it all felt so sensitive and arousing.

Jenny began to pluck at her nipples, gasping at the sensitivity, I was sure. I did the same pulling and pinching until my pussy began to cream.

As we touched ourselves, our breaths came faster and deeper.

When we were ready, we reached out to each other.

My hands cupped her firm mounds and she inhaled sharply at my touch. Her warm palms tenderly cupped my breasts, and I moaned as her thumbs rubbed my engorged nipples.

Then she leaned over, and I cried out as she sucked my hardened nipple into her succulent mouth. Her lips were plump and hot as she tenderly slurped. I moaned as I felt that little metal ball at the tip of her moist tongue smooth teasingly over my bud and then around my areole.

Her teeth gently nipped, making my nipple throb and my legs went weak from the intoxicating pleasure she so easily created. Gently she let go and then moved her mouth and hand away over to my other breast. With her fingers, she kneaded my flesh while brushing her thumb across my quivering bud. Then her hot mouth melted over my straining nipple, making me moan at the searing impact.

She tenderly bit my sensitive bud and then nibbled, sending pleasure waves cascading throughout my body. She slurped and sucked and slurped some more until I became heady with arousal.

We went on like this for quite some time and I became lost in the euphoria and then from somewhere I could hear Ashton's guttural cries. Could hear the slap of flesh against flesh. I was so enthralled with what Jenny was doing to me that I could barely open my eyes to see what was going on.

Shock penetrated my pleasure and I had to blink several times to make sure that what I was seeing was actually real.

I saw Dixon. He was naked and standing behind Ashton, who was bent over at the waist, his hands holding his ankles. Dixon's hands were firm on Ashton's hips and Dixon was thrusting his condom sheathed cock into a nude Ashton's ass.

Not only that, but I also saw Leo and he was plunging his engorged penis into Dixon's ass!

Oh my gosh! The sight of one man fucking another man who was fucking yet another man was something I had never imagined seeing before.

And all three of them were watching us!

Wow, they really got off on two women being together, didn't they?

Jenny seemed totally oblivious as to what was going on as she let go of my nipple with a huge pop and pulled her head away.

"Your turn," she whispered, and smiled endearingly.

Wow, yeah. She had a really pretty smile, and it did something genuinely nice to my lower belly.

I leaned down and saw that her nipples were rosy, and I could see a bit of milk glistening at the tips.

I licked off the milk, loving the moan she gave. It tasted of milky water, and I eagerly wrapped my lips around her tight bud and began to suckle from her breast. She hissed and groaned as I sucked, drawing milk.

Her fingers curled around my shoulders, and she pushed her chest against me.

"Harder, suck harder," she hissed.

So, I did, loving the pillowy curve of her breast as I buried my face against her flesh and adoring the way her hot nipple pulsated and jerked in my mouth. I relished in her soft moans of arousal; the sounds were like music to my ears.

Mercy, I could go on sucking and appreciating her gasps and moans forever and I could understand why some men would have the fetish of sucking milk from a women's breasts as if felt so intimate.

As Jenny and I enjoyed ourselves, I heard the men coming. Each of them gasping or groaning as they reached their orgasm.

Soon after, I heard one of them shout for us to stop.

Reluctantly, I let go of Jenny's nipple, and I could barely catch my breath at the way her heavy-lidded gaze stared at me.

"It was wonderful," she whispered to me.

Then she pulled away from me and casually turned toward the three men who were hurriedly donning their clothing and then grabbing their weapons where they had sloppily tossed them to the ground in all directions around them.

Hmm, this was interesting.

Watching two women touching each other truly made these men careless. I would have to be on guard for possible escape attempts from here on out.

BY QUITTING TIME, I was wiped out from all the fresh air, sunshine and walking behind that noisy tractor and listening to the cheerful chatter of the guards who kept commenting on how hot Jenny and I had looked with each other while they'd had sex.

Personally, all I wanted to do was get back to my cell and rest. My baby bump felt heavier than usual, and my breasts felt so engorged since having Jenny's hands on them, that I could just scream with wanting hands touching there again.

But the prison guards appeared to have other plans as they herded the two of us to the van that was to take us back to the prison, but no one made a move to put on our restraints or to open the van door.

Instead, Dixon held a clipboard in his hand. Acting all professional as he called out Jenny's name.

Good heavens! Roll call? Was he for real?

"Here," she said, rolling her eyes at me.

Then he called out my name.

I didn't answer. Instead, I just stared at him as irritation fumed through me.

He peered up from the clipboard and passed me a stern look that sent warning signals down my spine. We had been taught to always say the word here when a guard did roll call. Yet they had never done it with just me and why the hell do it with the two of us standing right here in front of them.

Like seriously?

"Are you being subordinate?" Dixon asked.

"I don't know. Am I?" I quipped enjoying the heated look he was throwing me.

"Maybe she needs little reminder of whom is in charge?" Dixon 's hand went to his belt buckle.

I trembled with excitement.

Oh yes, some sexy punishment might take the edge off my irritation and make the rest of my day.

"Turn around, Mad," Dixon instructed as he unzipped his fly.

I hesitated and held my breath wanting to see his shaft spring free of his pants.

"Hey man, if you delay us, Dixon, there might be trouble," Leo cautioned.

To my surprise, Dixon stopped and then walked toward the back of the van we'd arrived in. He pulled out his beating stick and struck the taillight. Plastic crackled. He hit the taillight again and red plastic flew everywhere.

"We've already left. Give us fifteen minutes and then Dixon and I will come back when you call to say the prison van is unsafe because you inadvertently backed it into a tree," Ashton surmised as he also went for his belt.

Leo chuckled, catching on that Dixon and Ashton were setting up an alibi for why they would be back late to the prison.

"Okay, but I'm not one for watching when others get their pleasure."

"We'll all watch each other," Dixon replied.

My pussy creamed as Dixon nodded to Jenny.

"Mad is mine and Jenny is here for something as you well know," he said to Leo.

I blew out a very tense breath and found it extremely exciting that I might be able to see Jenny having sex.

"Alright, ladies. You heard the man. Both of you get naked. Face the van, bend over, and show us your cute asses," Ashton said in a hoarse voice.

I shook my head.

"Not until we negotiate, boys."

Dixon chuckled as he began to remove his weapons.

"Wouldn't want it any other way, Queen. Your wish is our command."

Hmm, I liked this accommodating side of the man who'd fathered my child.

I turned to Jenny.

"Jenny. Is this okay with you?"

She nodded.

"Sign me up," she replied with a grin.

"Working condoms, please, gentlemen. And tomorrow, Jenny and I will watch you men work, all day."

Ashton looked at Dixon. And then at Leo.

Both men nodded with wide smiles on their faces.

"But both of you are naked and you'll play with yourselves and each other whenever we ask for a show," Dixon interjected.

I inhaled slowly as I thought about it. Then I gazed at Jenny, who winked affirmation.

"Weather permitting, agreed," I answered.

"And we'll talk more about what else, tomorrow," Dixon said.

Just the thought of having sex with Dixon and Ashton again had me creaming. And I hoped Leo would be added to the mix. I shouldn't be feeling this way regarding a man who I suspected had gotten me pregnant on purpose, but this situation certainly wasn't normal.

Hell, I wasn't normal, and I was thrilled to get some sexual release. From the quick way Jenny was undressing, she appeared excited as well.

Chapter Seven

I inhaled sharply as moments later I stood naked, facing the van, my upper body bent over and forward. My palms were pressed against the side of the vehicle for support.

I hissed and my pussy clenched as Dixon's warm body curled over me and he pressed himself against my back as he reached down, his hot hands scorching a trail over my big baby bump before coming up to cup my big breasts.

"Your body is luscious, my Queen. A vessel for my pleasure. I love you this way, plump and pregnant," he commented in a low aroused voice as he intimately massaged my tender flesh, bringing an incredible wash of vibrations into me. He was tweaking my nipples and I suddenly realized he was actually trying to milk me like a cow.

I gazed down and watched his thumb and middle finger pulling on my nipple as liquid dripped from my swollen tips.

"You'll be milked by me tomorrow, Mad. You'll be nourishing me and giving me strength to fuck you. You like that don't you, baby?" he groaned.

I nodded, feeling almost euphoric at the thought of him sucking me dry, and pleasuring me.

At the same time, his hot, firm cockhead was dipping into my eager vagina, collecting my creamy vaginal juices for lube, and then he pulled out to teasingly massage my throbbing clitoris.

Sensations whipped through me at his intimate touches.

From beside me I heard Jenny whimper. I gazed over just in time to watch her mouth drop open in a silent cry as Leo swiftly launched his condom sheathed cock into her. She was in the same position as I was in, so I don't know if he was taking her vaginally or anally.

But her face was scrunched up in utter pleasure as he pistoned.

"Very nice, Mad. Your pussy is sweet and wet. And so perfectly responsive," Dixon muttered as he slowly slid his thick, long shaft into my tightening vagina.

I could feel his every pulsing inch as he penetrated me. Could feel the elevated veins and the scorching heat from his ultra-rigid cock.

I didn't answer him as I kept my gaze to Jenny's face loving how her cheeks were now flushed red as she moved with every buck from Leo. She was keening and the sound aroused me, making me quite aware of Dixon's cock penetrating my body.

Instinctively I angled my hips further back allowing for a deeper penetration.

Dixon went deeper and yeah, he fit so perfectly.

The mild spring air whispered against my heated body as Dixon withdrew and then he began thrusting, making sure his pelvic bone nicely nailed my engorged clitoris.

Oh man, he made me feel so good.

I quickly embraced the pleasure and then I felt an unusually forceful buck of Dixon's body against mine. Instinctively I knew Ashton was getting in on the action., taking Dixon from behind.

Dixon's thrusts grew faster, harder, pushing the pleasure deeper into me and then suddenly I convulsed as an agonizing climax roared through me like a tornado.

My cries shattered the air as muscles in my pussy, ass, and lower abdomen, sweetly contracted and then spasmed, unleashing waves of ecstasy. I swirled into bliss and keened as each shudder snapped through me like live wires of electricity.

The bucks against me increased, and I knew Dixon and Ashton were nearing their own release.

I kept my gaze focused on Jenny.

Her eyes were tightly closed, and she was gasping up a storm, gyrating like a maniac as she also soared into her apex.

Man, this was insanely beautiful, I thought as spasms continued wrenching into me.

The five of us having sex, outdoors. It was all so illegal.

And yet so titillating.

"THERE'S MORE PUNISHMENT where that came from if you ladies don't behave," Dixon muttered as a little while later he slid open his van door.

Leo was on the radio letting the prison know about the issue with the other van, that we had been delayed, and that we would be arriving with Ashton and Dixon.

I said nothing about Dixon's comment as I followed Jenny into the van.

A moment later, we were cuffed to the metal bench, and then Dixon was gone.

"They can dole out that kind of punishment anytime," Jenny said beneath her breath.

I glanced up at her to find her cheeks were still flushed an incredible red and she had a cute smile on her ruby red lips.

"So, this is what you were experiencing before you escaped? Gosh, woman, why did you ever leave? And how? They are armed to the teeth."

"I'd rather not talk about it at the moment," I answered tightly.

I was still reeling from my orgasm. It had been so intense that my pussy continued to spasm even after all this time. I was also struggling with craving to have another cock penetrating me.

"Sure, sorry," Jenny said softly.

"Thanks," I nodded.

Truth be told, I also didn't want to discuss why I'd escaped. That I had feared for my and my baby's life. I had been afraid Dixon and Ashton would kill me once they found out I was pregnant. But it appeared that had just been a fear. I mean, why would Dixon impregnate me on purpose if he had, and then kill me? There had also been a comment from the other inmate I'd gotten pissed off at this morning when she'd suggested I'd be beating up my baby's sibling.

If it was true and Dixon was going around impregnating female prisoners, then Dixon was just an overconfident, crazy guard who had an extreme fetish for pregnant women. And because he was so arrogant, just like Leo and Ashton, they must honestly think they would not get caught.

Man, they really did have balls, so to speak.

Well, that was okay. I'd enjoyed the sex, fresh air, and Jenny's company. And I couldn't wait until tomorrow!

I SPENT THE EVENING resting.

My belly continued to feel heavy and so did my breasts. I wished I could have Jenny's lips sucking on my nipples again or Dixon's hands milking me.

Gosh, today out on the fields had felt forbidden, yet so erotic.

I smiled and wondered how tomorrow was going to play out. I'd have to figure out a way to request a triple penetration by the guards without them cluing in that's what I wanted because I sure didn't want them to get the power over me instead of the other way around.

Tonight, supper had been surprisingly delicious.

Juicy steak, mashed potatoes, fresh vegetables, and a Coke in a can, which was rare.

I had the feeling one of the guards had set it up to sweeten the deal for tomorrow.

For dessert, I nibbled on more of those devilish chocolates Leo had dropped into my cell the night he'd watched me masturbate.

Later in the evening, as the lights dimmed for the night, excitement rushed through me as a little while later, as I lay in my cot beneath the blanket, I heard footsteps coming down the hall. I held my breath as the Peeping Tom window slid open and to my disappointment, a moment later, it slid closed.

I had hoped Leo was returning with another box of chocolates to watch me masturbate but the footsteps echoed away, and silence followed.

The thought of pleasuring myself crossed my mind, but I decided against it. I figured I needed my rest for whatever naughtiness transpired tomorrow.

I turned onto my side, felt a little kick, and lovingly hugged my baby bump.

Soon, my baby would be born, and he or she would be free of this place. When that day of us parting came, it would be heartbreaking for sure.

But I didn't want my baby behind bars if I could help it.

I closed my eyes and prayed that somehow, I would be able to get outside these walls right along with my baby.

Wishful thinking? Perhaps, but the thought of leaving with my baby brought happiness to my heart.

I slept.

THE NEXT MORNING EAGERNESS zipped through me as I met Jenny in the outfitting room where we picked out jumpsuits, gloves, and boots.

She seemed pretty cheerful as we ignored the other pregnant prisoners who heckled and talked dirty about us being the guards' favorite sluts.

I did not like being made fun of and my anger was just about to the boiling point when Jenny touched my elbow.

I gazed at her, and her serene smile diffused a retort I was about to fling at the prisoners. I had already decided I would smash in the loudest woman's nose if she didn't shut up.

"Don't you want to have a pleasant workday?" Jenny muttered and winked.

I nodded and felt some of my anger diffuse.

She was right.

I glared at the females who laughed and made even more crude remarks, but I held onto my temper.

Those stupid bitches weren't worth my getting an extended length in solitary.

"Jenny and Mad, this way please," Leo called out and waved us over.

He was standing in the doorway, grinning like the cat who ate the canary as we approached him.

"Good morning, ladies. Are you ready for another excruciating hard day of labor?" Leo called out.

He was talking exceptionally loudly, so I figured he wanted the other inmates to hear what he had to say. And they were listening because the group of women that had been heckling Jenny and I had suddenly gone silent.

The other guard who'd been carefully watching me yesterday while Leo had shackled us, was quietly watching me again, his hand hovering over his taser gun expecting trouble as Leo slipped on our restraints.

"I'm surprised you ladies aren't more tired with the workout we gave you yesterday," Leo said with a maniacal laugh.

My face warmed as I remembered the naughty things Jenny and I had done with each other yesterday while the guards had watched and then how we'd both been punished and taken by the guards near the van before leaving for the prison.

The inmates continued to watch us, but all remained quiet. Even that other guard was quiet.

Sheesh! What was up with that guy? He creeped me out with the distrust looming look in his dark eyes. I'd never had a guard look at me like I was actually someone to be afraid of. I mean sure the guards were all cautious, it was a prison, but something was off about him. I did not like the vibes he was giving off.

Jenny smiled at Leo as he held the door open for us and we hobbled along, our chains rattling with each step. I was glad when I was out of that creepy guard's sight.

Moments later, Leo had us secured in the van and I was once again looking forward to this day.

"I cannot wait for another hard day of labor. Emphasis on hard," Jenny said in a low voice.

I caught the amusement in her eyes and found myself laughing out loud.

"Keep it down back there, ladies!" Leo shouted as he stepped into the van and took the driver seat.

"I certainly hope they *don't* keep it down or they'll never get it in back there," Jenny murmured cheerfully under her breath.

I got her teasing remarks. They better not be flaccid, or they would not be able to penetrate an ass. Once again, I couldn't stop myself from laughing out loud.

"If you don't quieten down, I'll give you something to be happy about," Leo growled.

He caught my gaze in the rearview mirror, and I inhaled at his heated look.

Oh boy, he was primed for sex today and so was I.

Chapter Eight

I tossed him a wink, and he reluctantly returned his attention to driving the van out of the prison garage and into the bright sunshine.

"You're quite cheerful, today," I commented as Jenny continued to smile at me.

"Why wouldn't I be? A full day of no work outdoors would make anyone happy. Not to mention the fringe benefits. I enjoyed our kiss yesterday and if I may say you have beautiful breasts. I can't wait to see them again. And just so you know I am bisexual, and I am quite attracted to you," she complimented in a soft voice so that Leo couldn't hear.

Oh my, she was being so bold this morning.

To my surprise, my cheeks heated as I remembered what we had done while the guards had watched.

"I enjoyed it too," I replied truthfully.

Man, I had never expected to be into a woman or have one into me. But I think I was beginning to have feelings for her. She calmed me and she made me feel special in an intimate way. And yeah, I really did like her sweet smile and the interested way she looked at me.

"Leo seems to be in a bit of a frustrated mood this morning," Jenny said as she smoothed her hand over her bulging baby bump.

"I hope he wasn't too rough on you, yesterday?" I asked, remembering how he had entered her fast and furious.

"Oh, no, I enjoy sex with Leo. He took my ass, and it was quite forceful, but he knows I like it that way."

My curiosity was piqued.

"How often have you and Leo…?"

"Oh, since shortly after I arrived here. He came to my cell one night, dropped in a box of really expensive chocolate and proceeded to masturbate while watching me do the same," Jenny replied.

"You're kidding?" Of course, she wasn't kidding, as the same thing had happened to me.

"That was my introduction to what goes on behind prison bars."

"Really. And he's been having sex with you ever since?"

"Yes. I was shy at first. But he can be quite insistent. You know being behind bars you really have nowhere to run if you don't like that kind of attention."

"Did you want to run? At first, I mean." I asked.

The idea that poor Jenny was being badgered for sex by Leo pissed me off. I was feeling protective of her, just like I had been yesterday.

"Well, maybe. I mean, I'm not used to doing illegal stuff. But I have found out it can be quite exciting and fulfilling."

"Fulfilling? That's an odd thing to say about illegal activities," I commented.

Jenny's smile widened and she shrugged her shoulders.

"I didn't mean that I got off on doing illegal things. I meant it appears I have a voyeurism side. I get off knowing people are watching when I'm having sex. Like yesterday. I knew you were watching, and I was so aroused."

I wanted to tell her that I felt the same way. That I'd enjoyed watching her have sex with Leo, but I kept quiet. I didn't want her knowing my feelings. I barely knew her. And I sure wasn't going to take this attraction I had to her seriously. At least not yet.

We both fell silent into our own thoughts as we gazed out the van windows.

Bright sunshine glinted off the silver silos near a farmhouse in the distance and big black cows wandered around in a muddy field. As the miles flew by, we passed a couple of chain gangs of women dressed in orange jumpers who were raking leaves and picking garbage out of the ditches of the solitary highway.

Then my heart began to speed up as Leo finally turned the van off the highway onto the farmers lane and a little while later, he turned down another lane.

Before long I spied the other prison van, with Dixon and Ashton standing there waiting for us. Dixon was holding that clipboard in his hand. I trembled as I remembered what had happened the last time he'd held that clipboard.

"Hmm, it looks like it's showtime," Jenny commented with a smile as she stared at them.

My pulse began to frantically pound as I suddenly remembered what I had agreed to yesterday regarding more one on one with Jenny while the guards watched as well as Dixon requiring other things for us to do.

Rolls of eagerness ripped through me and I was trembling as a few moments later Jenny and I stepped out of the van and Leo instructed us to stand before Dixon.

"Good morning, ladies," Dixon said. He spoke in a professional voice but in the way his pants were tented between his thighs, he was already aroused.

"We'll do roll call and then get right to work," Dixon said as he gazed down at his clipboard.

I wondered if he were maybe wanting me to refuse to answer roll call like I did yesterday so they could punish us again. I decided not to play that game today. I didn't want to come off as predictable.

He called out Jenny's name and she quickly answered.

He called out my name and I hesitated for just a few seconds, until he looked up and flashed his blue eyes at me as if daring me not to answer.

"Here," I said in a firm no-nonsense voice.

Did I detect disappointment in his gaze?

I smiled inwardly.

Dixon checked off my name and then tossed the clipboard into the van, closing the passenger door with an exceptionally loud bang.

Yup, he'd definitely thought I wouldn't answer and that he would be punishing me again.

That I'd disappointed him made me feel good and powerful.

Ashton told us to follow him into the rows of spruce trees that lined the farmer's lane. Dixon and Leo came up close behind me. I felt excited hearing their heavy breathing, but a bit pissed that they followed so closely. Like seriously, we were still in our wrist and ankle restraints. We weren't going anywhere.

The spruce trees gave way to the same field we'd been working in yesterday and we stopped by the tractor with attached seeding machine. There was a new and larger amount of bagged corn stacked nearby. The sun was shining brilliantly in a clear blue sky and thankfully the spring breeze was fresh and warm.

"As per our agreement yesterday," Dixon paused and stared right at me. His blue eyes sparkled with excitement.

"We want to see the two of you naked, while we work. So, time to show us your assets."

Jenny was as always obedient and made a move to lower her jumper zipper, but I reached out and grabbed her wrist, stopping her. The sounds of our chains clinked through the air.

"Hold on, gentlemen," I said in a stern voice. All three men moaned.

I smiled inwardly. These men were obviously so hooked on us which I of course planned to use to our advantage.

"What do you want, our Queen?" Ashton asked. There was a small smile on his otherwise severe expression.

"First of all, we can't undress with all this metal hanging off us," I said.

I held out my hands and the chains rattled.

Obviously in their excitement they'd forgotten we couldn't get naked with our restraints on.

Dixon nodded to Leo, who quickly located his keys. A few minutes later, we were free of all manacles.

What an awesome feeling to not have those heavy weights on my limbs and the clattering noise of them grinding on my nerves.

"What else do you want?" Dixon grumbled as Jenny, and I made no move to undress.

Good girl, I silently complimented her. She was catching on.

My heart picked up speed at what I was about to propose.

"After our two-hour lunch, I would like to suggest you three men all get naked."

I loved their inhalations of surprise and held my breath, wondering how far I could take this.

Would they submit to being without their clothing and their weapons? Would they allow the two-hour lunch I'd snuck in there?

"And I will tell you what I want you men to do. It is only fair that if you watch us play with each other, we get to watch you do certain things to each other."

The three men gazed at one another. It was as if they were sending secret messages between them.

I read their body language. Their eyes were flashing with enthusiasm and their bodies were tense with arousal. Just looking between their legs at their tented pants gave their anticipation away.

Then Ashton spoke.

"On one condition," he said.

Shoot, they always had to one up it, didn't they.

"What would that be?"

"Afterwards, *you* bring us release while Jenny watches," Ashton replied.

Man, this was really turning me on!

I swallowed and tried hard not to show my extreme interest.

"All three of you taking me? At once?" I said, pretending I was kind of frightened.

But wow, they were dropping my secret fantasy of triple penetration right into my lap!

I saw Dixon nodding.

I swore I just about came on the spot at their proposition.

I forced myself to calm down before answering, but I couldn't calm myself.

I was seriously aroused.

"Deal," I said in a very tight voice.

"Good. But first, you ladies will have to nourish us so we can work," Dixon said.

I trembled at his words and watched the tip of his tongue lick around his upper and then lower lip like he was about to get a really good treat. I knew exactly what he wanted. He wanted to suckle from my breasts.

The slow, seductive movement mesmerized me, and I suddenly couldn't wait for their mouths to be on my hardening nipples. I thought about bargaining with them, maybe getting longer breaks for today, but we didn't have any breaks today because we weren't working.

Suddenly I just didn't want to waste another minute not having their lips at my heavy breasts.

Jenny was looking at me for direction. Obviously, she expected me to continue negotiating, but I just nodded to her, and we began to undress in front of the three guards who eagerly watched us.

Chapter Nine

Moments later, Jenny and I stood naked in front of the men. Our big pregnant bellies and our large breasts kept their gaze's hostage as they stared at us. I noticed the ground was cold and damp beneath my bare feet, but I'd slip on my socks and shoes later. Thankfully, the rest of me felt scrumptiously hot beneath the scorching way they were watching us.

I felt no shame. I was comfortable with my body. Knew how to use it to get me what I wanted and at the moment I wanted them.

My pussy and ass were clenching up a storm as Dixon and Leo moved toward me, and Ashton strolled toward Jenny.

"I've been waiting to taste your luscious nipples again, my Queen," Dixon said, his blue eyes flashing with need.

"I've been waiting to taste them ever since I saw those juicy lollipops back in solitaire," Leo murmured. He'd removed his glasses and placed them into his shirt pocket. An eager expression was plastered onto his face as he admired my milk-laden breasts.

"When was this?" he asked, obviously knowing Leo wasn't talking about yesterday when the three of them had taken Jenny and me by the van.

Dixon was frowning.

Hmm, did I detect a bit of jealousy?

"Sorry man, but a gentleman doesn't tattle on his Queen," Leo replied with a smile.

Dixon chuckled and his focus returned to my breasts.

"Man, but aren't those nipples pretty?" Dixon murmured.

"They sure are and they belong to us. These ladies belong to us, and I can't wait until we get them pregnant again," Leo answered.

I was too aroused to take much insight to what Leo was saying. But somewhere in the naughty part of my mind, I did kind of want to be pregnant again by one of these guards. To have the men watch my body blossom with child because they'd missed out after I'd escaped.

I knew I had to be crazy thinking in such a defiling way, but the idea of getting pregnant again did arouse me.

My breaths came quicker at that thought and even faster as both men stepped closer to me.

Immediately beside me I heard Jenny whimper, and I looked over to see that she was staring at me with intense need on her face. Her lips were parted with heavy pants, while Ashton had already cupped her large breasts in his palms and his mouth moved rhythmically as he sucked on her right nipple.

Gosh, the expression of pleasure splashing across her face had me wanting to kiss her.

Since we were standing close enough to each other, she must have been reading my mind, because before I knew it our heads leaned closer to each other, and our lips touched.

Sparks of arousal flew through my mouth as we kissed each other. Her tongue quickly darted between my parted lips and mated with mine, thrusting against my tongue like a seductive mini cock.

I moaned at the heady sensations her kiss created and then arched as Dixon and Leo cupped my breasts, their eager lips wrapping around my turgid, sensitive nipples.

Dixon sucked in hard motions, while Leo was a bit less intense, gentler. But the combination was perfect.

Their male scents swarmed around my senses, and I gasped into Jenny's mouth when moments later a strong hand slid between my parted naked thighs.

Instinctively I knew it was Dixon who was touching my pussy and I trembled as his finger dipped into my vagina and then withdrew. Then a wet finger began to leisurely rub my engorged clitoris making my abdomen tighten as pleasure waves spiralled through me.

Oh my gosh! I could just imagine how I looked to anyone coming upon this scene.

Two naked, very pregnant women, standing beside each other, kissing each other while three men suckled milk from their breasts.

All this mental and visual stimulation was making me so unbelievably aroused.

I reached up and curled my hands over their muscular shoulders while their lips sucked and nibbled and then ever so slowly, I could feel the heavy pressure leaving my breasts as they drained milk from me, leaving my nipples amazingly sensitive to their every suck.

Oh, it all felt incredibly good.

And the intoxicating way Jenny's mouth made love to mine was exhilarating. She truly knew how to kiss.

The finger rubbing my clit moved faster and faster, unleashing carnal shudders that had me bucking and keening. The sucking on my nipples grew stronger and stronger. Their hot mouths pulled and slurped and then my world suddenly rocked as a climax slammed into me, spinning me into a wicked world of spasms.

I had become two nipples, a pussy, and lips.

That's all I could feel as I slowly ebbed out of my shuddering climax.

Dixon and Leo's sucking and slurping mouths were slowing, and Jenny's kiss had become intimate and gentle as she pushed that gold piercing at the tip of her tongue against the tip of my tongue. It was a beautiful after orgasm kiss that had me moaning my appreciation.

My vagina continued to clench around Dixon's fingers, but the luscious spasms were quickly disappearing. And he'd slowed his drives, indicating the men were almost finished with me.

But I sure would love to have another orgasm, I thought with joy.

Was I being greedy? Heck no. I just enjoyed orgasms. Always had.

I whimpered my disappointment as Dixon withdrew his fingers from my vagina. Soon the two men stopped suckling and they pulled away.

My nipples throbbed from having their mouths sucking on them, but my breasts felt wonderful. They felt light and properly milked, the heaviness I'd been feeling lately, was gone.

Jenny stopped her kisses and then pulled away. Her eyes glowed with arousal as she looked at me. Obviously, she had enjoyed herself too.

I dropped my gaze to Ashton, who was moving his lips from Jenny's burgeoning nipple.

For a split second I realized I had access to his weapons. Heck, I'd had access to all their weapons, but I'd been too aroused to even think about grabbing one.

I'd been an idiot. Another lost opportunity. But I sensed there would be more chances in the future, especially with them being so careless.

None of the men gave us any thanks as they hurried away, returning to the pile of seed bags. They began chatting and laughing as they broke open the sacks of corn seed and dumped the contents into the seeder.

I guess our milk had cheered them up and nourished them quite nicely because they were moving rather fast as they talked nonstop. Maybe they figured since the winter had been so long and the warm weather so slow in coming this year, it was time to get their asses in gear.

To my surprise, Jenny grabbed my hand and led me over to where there were a couple of lawn chairs that had been placed at the edge of the field. Folded fleece blankets were set upon the seats.

Huh, why hadn't I seen this set up when we had first arrived? Probably because I'd been so excited, that's why.

"Just don't cover up. We want to see all of you," Ashton shouted a reminder.

Jenny waved acknowledgement.

I blew out a tense breath as we grabbed the blankets and draped them over the chairs. I also retrieved our socks and shoes. Then after putting them on, we sat on the lawn chairs and watched them work, both of us quiet.

Jenny was probably processing what had just happened like I was doing.

Wow, but the experience of having her kissing me with two men sucking milk from my breasts and getting aroused by Dixon's fingers had been powerful. I could get used to these sexual adventures. But I now also began to remember what Leo had said earlier.

His comment about making us pregnant *again* had me coming up with some questions. Leo's confession was another notch toward my suspicion that I had been impregnated on purpose all those months ago. Which made me wonder, what about Jenny?

I had assumed her baby was her husband's baby.

"Jen? Who is the father of your baby?" I blurted. Suddenly I just had to know.

She had been watching the men, a smile on her face and when I asked the question, her smile only brightened. She turned to me and winked.

"It's a secret," she whispered.

"The baby is not your husband's?" I asked.

She said nothing. Just stared at me as if I weren't getting something.

Oh gosh, I was being too meddlesome. It really was none of my business, but my curiosity kept pushing me.

"How long have you been at this prison?" I asked.

She might have been here for quite some time as prisoners in different cell blocks rarely saw one another.

"A little over nine months," she replied, and I noticed she was gently caressing her baby bump.

Well, there, I had my answer.

That's why she'd been looking at me kind of funny. This kid was not her husband's kid. It took time to go through the court system to get to prison. That meant she had lost that last baby too, after her husband had beat her and she'd shot him.

How had she managed to stay sane with a nut job husband like that and losing so many kids?

"How far along are you anyway? I asked.

"A little over nine months," she answered.

"Wow, they didn't waste any time with you, did they?" I snapped.

My protective instincts for Jenny were coming out again.

She shrugged her shoulders making her big breasts bounce.

"I wanted to carry a baby to term. In here I can do that. The guards are good to me. They don't hit me," she explained.

Man, I felt bad for her.

Having a kid in prison just wasn't the way to go, couldn't she see that? Maybe she had taken too many blows to the head from her asshole husband that she couldn't see having a baby here was a bad idea. It would be yanked away from her and put into someone else's care. It was going to break her heart.

I mean, I got that she might feel protected here, especially after all the abuse she'd endured from her husband, but seriously? Did she not understand the guards were abusing us by pursing us in the first place, having sex and impregnating us? That all of this was illegal?

I wanted to tell Jenny to give her head a shake, but I realized I would be a hypocrite if I said that because I was enjoying the sex too. I mean I could have said no to the guards right at the start, but I hadn't. I'd used their interest in me to my advantage. And I could have tipped off the cops after I had escaped. But I hadn't.

So, I guess I shouldn't throw stones, right?

"Is the baby, Leo's?" I asked, remembering that she had admitted Leo knew how she liked to be taken anally.

Jenny giggled playfully.

"You're not going to stop asking, are you?"

Chapter Ten

"To tell you the truth, I am like a dog with a bone. When I get something in my head, I cannot let it go."

She sighed and shook her head.

"I'm not sure who the father is. But that doesn't mean I don't love this baby because I really do. I've been given another chance to become a mother and I took it."

Oh, man.

"They used condoms. But sometimes the condoms broke and then I was pregnant," she said innocently.

Gee, major surprise there. Not.

I wondered if the kid was Dixon's. At that thought I felt my baby give me a swift kick.

I gasped at the niggle of pain it created and then slowly blew out a tense breath. The baby was quiet again.

Gosh, I hoped my kid wasn't trying to tell me that yes, he or she had plenty of siblings in this prison atmosphere.

"How many guards did you have sex with?"

She shrugged and looked hurt that I would ask her such a question.

"They always bring me to orgasm, and I enjoy it. Why so many questions?" she asked, frowning. Her frown made me feel guilty.

"Sorry. I guess it's none of my business."

"You're not thinking of ratting them out to the authorities, are you?" she said in a serious tone.

"Oh gosh, no. I don't need that kind of attention." I said, truthfully.

Hell, no one would believe me anyway and how could I even report them? And to who? The warden was probably in on it.

She was still staring at me, maybe even studying me as if trying to figure out if I really might rat everyone out.

"Besides, I enjoy the sex too," I added.

"So, why would I want to screw up a good thing? I am the Queen after all." I joked, hoping to alleviate the weird tension that I felt zipping off her.

I shouldn't have pried into her business. I should have kept my mouth shut.

Now I was afraid that Jenny might say something to one of the guards, and then I would be screwed if they thought their little house of pregnant prisoners was in trouble.

"Why don't we just sit back and enjoy how the rest of the day unfolds," Jenny suggested.

She appeared to be relaxed again and I noticed she'd begun to caress the nipple that Ashton had sucked on.

I followed her gaze to the guards. They were observing us from beside the tractor. Their stares were hot and filled with anticipation.

It appeared Jenny wanted to put on a show for them and they were quite eager to watch.

"Do me while they watch," she whispered.

I didn't understand what she meant and then she opened her legs.

"Oh," I replied.

I smiled.

It was showtime.

Slowly I got up off the lawn chair and walked around to stand in front of Jenny. She was gazing up at me, her eyes filled with elation. She whimpered when I got down on my hands and knees between her spread legs.

Her baby belly was hanging low blocking my view of her pussy, so I asked her to scoot forward on the lawn chair. She did as I instructed and there it appeared, her labia plump and glistening with juices. I even caught a glint of gold as she spread her legs wider.

Her mons was nude, and I wondered if she shaved there or if it was a permanent removal of her pubic hair at the demand of her crazy husband. She also had a piercing. Actually, two piercings. A small gold ring hung near the end of each labium. Her pussy lips were huge and quite long, as if they'd been over stretched.

My mouth watered and my vagina grew hot at the thought of taking those plump pussy lips into my mouth.

"My husband would hang weights from them to punish me. It hurt and then sometimes it was erotic, but right now I need some soothing down there, especially after watching what the men just did to you," she whispered in a thick voice.

Wow, that husband of hers really did put her through some not nice stuff. I pushed aside thoughts of the bastard as empathy for her rocked through me.

Of course, I should have known she would be aroused at watching what had happened. She needed to be brought to some satisfaction because it was cruel having her watch and then not bringing her pleasure to completion.

"I'll make you feel so much better, Jenny," I said softly.

Her breathing was rough and fast as I dipped my head forward and then I angled my face toward her pussy.

I placed my hands upon Jenny's knees and held them apart. A moment later, Jenny cried out as my mouth melted over her quaking pussy and I could feel her shudder as I began a gentle sucking.

This was my first time going down on a woman, and for a few frantic seconds, I didn't know what to do. Then I realized what an incredible advantage I had. I was a woman, and I knew all our erogenous zones, so I could arouse Jenny and I would use my tongue and my teeth!

Keeping my mouth fused over her pussy, I tenderly lapped her labium, then her moist clitoris and enjoyed her quickening breaths and the tightening of her thighs.

Then I sipped gently on the sensitive bundle of nerves, feeling the heat of her clit hot on my tongue.

I listened for her reaction and when I heard a soft moan, I shifted my mouth from her clit and slurped in a pussy lip, enjoying the contrast of the warm plumpness of her flesh and the coolness of the metal ring piercing.

Then I let go of her lip, sucking the other one into my mouth.

I licked her flesh and then pulled on the ring with my teeth until she whimpered. Then I let go, smiling as I dipped my tongue into her vagina. Her pussy muscles clenched around my tongue, and I could feel she was really drenched, meaning she was incredibly aroused.

"Oh! So nice," she hissed and thrust her fingers into my hair, holding tight enough to breathe pain across my scalp.

Hearing her approval, I slowly withdrew my tongue from her vagina and then began to lap her clitoris with long, steady strokes, until she was moaning in delight. Then I played with her labia again, pulling on her pussy rings, until her lips stretched, and she was keening.

Wow, I sure did love the different noises she made with my every touch. She sounded like erotic music.

I brought my lips over her hot clitoris again, and used my tongue to lick and lap until she was squirming.

It was so amazing how I could control her arousal.

My mouth moved to explore her plump pussy lips again. I sucked on both of them and nibbled and tugged until her warm cream gushed down her vagina and against my tongue.

Jenny's breaths were coming faster, and her thighs were shuddering magnificently against my head as I continued seducing her labia, then licking her clitoris, and then thrusting my tongue into her pussy like a miniature cock, making her moans grow louder and her keening longer.

I quickened my licks and laps and drank cream from her body.

Then she was crying out, her thighs clenching around my head, her body writhing like a maniacal rag doll on the lawn chair.

In the background, I could hear the guards whooping and urging me on, obviously enjoying our show.

Jenny screamed as she came.

The fingers tightening fiercely in my hair, as she bucked. She kept crying out, and I kept thrusting my tongue into her vagina, withdrawing to take quick jabs at her swelling clit, then driving back into her vagina again, all the while loving the spasms of all her clenching muscles.

I kept manipulating her clit, pussy lips and vagina until her orgasm ebbed and she was panting with satisfaction.

I waited until she let go of my hair before I moved from between her legs and gazed up at her. My breath halted at the sleepy, satisfied look in her heavy-lidded gaze.

Her smile of appreciation made my heart smile.

"That was magnificent. Thank you," she whispered.

"Hey, all in a day's work," I teased as I slowly got to my feet.

I wished for a warm, soapy washcloth to clean the stickiness from between her legs, but that wasn't available. Instead, I wet a corner of one of the extra fleece blankets with some cold drinking water. We waited until the guards returned to work, and the wet blanket became warm under the sunshine. Then Jenny wiped herself to freshness.

"I've never experienced something like that with another woman before," she said calmly as we leaned back in the lawn chairs, watching the guards toil in the field.

"Neither have I," I whispered.

Suddenly all I wanted to do was kiss Jenny again and bring her more arousal, but I held myself back.

The day was long, and we needed to save our energy in order to give more shows to the guards.

And just like clockwork the guards demanded a show about every half an hour, so we obliged as per the agreement. Jenny and I took turns kissing each other's body, touching our breasts, and caressing our intimate parts. She went down on me once and then we kissed some more, her sexy little mouth and that incredible tongue with the piercing turning me on to new heights wherever she touched.

The prison guards watched to the two of us having sex with huge smiles on their faces and big bulges tenting their pants. They were incredibly aroused, and I felt fevered as I imagined eventually bringing all three of them relief with my body.

Chapter Eleven

To my surprise, at lunch, Dixon presented us with hot steaks on kaisers and garden salads. Plus, more pop. I loved the sweetness of the drink and swore the minute I broke out of prison again I would buy pop for myself every day, remembering the day I was triple-penetrated.

When Dixon walked away, he said he'd see us in two hours. They had allowed the extra hour for lunch that I had thrown in during discussions this morning. How cool was that.

Jenny and I were jovial as we devoured our food while we sat naked beneath the gorgeous, warm spring sunshine. I truly felt like a queen with my cheerful pregnant companion by my side.

"Do you think you will try to escape again?" Jenny suddenly asked as she wiped her pretty mouth with a napkin after she finished her salad.

"I don't know," I answered.

"If you do, will you take me with you? I don't want to be apart from my baby."

Shit.

She was gazing at me with serious intent.

How the hell do I answer that question?

I was used now to doing things solo, but protecting Jenny was an emotion that was so thick and raw that it actually hurt, but in a good way.

Besides, the baby she was caring could be a sibling to my baby.

Man, the stakes of escaping just got higher. What could I tell her? The truth? Could I trust her? I didn't even know her. She could tattle on me, and then the guards would be on high alert.

"Sweetie, if I do decide to make a run for it somewhere down the line, of course I'll take you. But you need to keep it a secret, right?"

Jenny eagerly nodded, her hands flying to lovingly caress her big belly.

"Hear that baby? Your Auntie Maddie has given us hope. Someday we will be together again."

I smiled. Hope was always a good thing. Hope was what had kept me going through my years of prison.

Yeah, I would be escaping, but I would have to do it in the same way as the last time. Via a plan.

I needed to study the guards' routines and pick a time and a date to take off.

Hopefully, they would keep Jenny and I together until I decided to make another run for it. If not, then things would get complicated.

But for today, I was just going to relax and enjoy playing with the guards. My breaths quickened as I realized I would soon have my craving of being triple penetrated met by three generously hung men.

"WHAT IS YOUR WISH FOR us, oh Queen?" Leo asked as he was the first one to be fully naked and standing before Jenny and me at the end of our lunch time. He wore his glasses and I found he looked quite attractive wearing glasses while the rest of him was nude.

I could barely breathe from all my exhilaration, and I had to take several calming breaths to steady my rapid heartbeat before I dared to speak.

"My, oh, my, aren't you the eager one," I teased as I studied Leo's physique and felt myself falling deeper into a wonderous heat of arousal.

He was well built. His entire body nicely tanned. Either he went to a tanning booth, or he sunbathed nude. Every inch of the man looked hard and toned. He was a muscular man, just like Dixon and Ashton, who now flanked Leo.

Their erections were quite large. Jenny and I had truly turned them on with our shows for them.

Their penises were long and juicy thick. Big, muscular members that would pound into me with powerful thrusts, I was sure.

Leo's penis was a bit bigger and longer than the other two men and lust shone in all her eyes as they looked at me, eagerly awaiting instructions.

I blew out tense breaths as I reacted to their nakedness, the heat of arousal now exploding inside of me.

My breasts were feeling very heavy again, My nipples felt big, and they throbbed, eager for stimulation. My pussy was creaming, and my ass was clenching. Even my lips tingled with anticipation.

I resisted the urge to reach up and touch myself and put out the fires that were burning deep within me.

"I want each one of you to touch your cocks and follow my instructions, but do not bring yourself to completion. You will bring satisfaction to yourselves arousing my body when the time comes. Is that understood?" I said sternly.

I could hear the smokiness of enthusiasm in my voice. Could hear Jenny's breaths quicken at my words.

All three men moved in unison, their left hands moving to hold the base of their shafts. Their right hands stroking the length of their thick cocks.

I watched as Leo's fingers trailed along his swollen purplish scrotum and then underneath where he massaged himself there.

I felt my eyes widen as his shaft went longer and thicker and it just kept on growing!

My pussy trembled.

I wasn't sure if it was out of fear or from excitement as Leo's shaft just continued to grow right before my eyes.

Mercy, his size outshone the other two guards. But I knew size didn't matter, especially if a man knew how to arouse a woman. And these three men were arousing me just by my watching how their strong hands twisted and stroked their penises and cockheads.

I ached as they touched themselves and I felt a harsh thrum of blood rushing through my arteries making my body tighten with anticipation. I allowed them several more minutes to stroke themselves into mighty fine erections.

"Good boys. I love how beautiful your cocks have become. Nice and strong. Well done," I complimented.

The three men stared at me with heavy lidded eyes. Their lips were parted as they continued to caress themselves.

"Now, I want you men to put on a show for Jenny and I and I will give you the instructions. Dixon, I want you to go down on Leo. And Ashton, I want you to kiss Dixon's ass. Make sure you are all in positions where we can see everything you are doing."

The men eagerly nodded.

I knew Ashton had an ass fetish, so this command would turn him seriously on. And Dixon knew how to suck cock because he was enamored with Ashton and that was one of the ways the two men must pleasure each other. And well, I just wanted to watch Dixon suck Leo's big cock.

None of the men protested as they followed my instructions.

Leo turned to stand sideways, and Dixon came around and stood opposite of him. Then he dropped to his hands and knees, doggy style, in front of Leo.

"Good boys," I praised.

Dixon reached up and placed a hand at the base of Leo's pulsing purplish shaft. Eagerly, I watched as Dixon opened his mouth and angled his head toward Leo's long, thick erection. I blew out a tense breath as Dixon's mouth stretched over Leo's hard-looking flesh and I watched as about a third of Leo's cock disappeared into Dixon's mouth.

"Wow, Dixon has a big mouth. I didn't think he'd be able to accommodate, Leo. I mean I've tried, but he's just too big for my mouth," Jenny purred from beside me.

I nodded and for a few brief seconds I feared Leo's big cock might hurt me when the time came for his penetration into me, but then I sensed Leo would know how to go about pleasing a woman. I mean, I hadn't heard any complaints from Jenny with what she'd gone through with him yesterday.

So, I tried to calm myself to the best of my ability and focused my attention onto the three prison guards.

I watched as Leo's eyes scrunched up tight, pleasure whipping across his expression. He groaned as Dixon brought up his other hand and wrapped it about a third up from the base of Leo's shaft. I knew Dixon did this to prevent Leo's cock from entering his throat and evoking a gag reflex.

Then keeping his hands in position around Leo's shaft, Dixon moved his head backward bringing most of Leo's shaft out of his mouth.

"Good boy. Now, Dixon, I want you to prepare Leo for me. Make him nice and hot. But remember, don't let him come."

Dixon said nothing, and I watched as his lips tightened around Leo's turgid flesh.

He angled his head forward and about one third of Leo's shaft disappeared into Dixon's mouth. Leo began groaning as Dixon noisily slurped on his flesh.

Soon Dixon's head was moving backward and forward, faster, and faster, as he slipped Leo's cock in and out of his mouth.

Ashton was on his hands and knees behind Dixon, his lips noisily kissing Dixon's rounded ass cheeks.

I loved how my prison guards looked so erotic in their positions and they had been so obedient.

I enjoyed how Leo's mouth hung open, a twisted expression on his face as he panted, obviously enjoying what Dixon was doing to him. His fists were clenched while Dixon slurped on his plum-shaped cockhead, and then sucked part of his shaft into his mouth again.

I watched the men as they performed their show. Slurping and kissing sounds mingled with guttural groans and aroused inhalations. The three men just kept on going, obviously enjoying themselves immensely.

Dixon was in such a position that I was able to watch how his juicy, flushed cock hung down between his legs like that of a stallion. I truly had picked the right show for these men to perform for us because they were now so aroused, I wondered if they'd forgotten that I was here.

"Don't suck Leo too hard. And don't kiss Dixon's ass too much. I don't want any of you boys coming yet. Just remember that's what I am here for. To be pleasured by your glorious shafts. The Queen wants you to remember your erections are made for her," I teased as the heat of anticipation rushed throughout my body.

At my words, I noticed all three men had visibly tensed.

I realized that in the heat of their arousal they might have forgotten about me and that I had just reminded them that *I* was here for their release.

Oh well, I'd had my fun with them, and I valued how easily I'd been able to manipulate them into doing my bidding for them to put on a show for us. A feeling of power surged through my veins as I realized that when they were sexually excited, I could be the puppet master, and they, my obedient puppets.

But in the way their bodies remained tense, I sensed they would soon be paying their attention upon me, and I was right.

Ashton was the first to break free of the male trio.

"Oh, oh, here comes one," Jenny squealed under her breath and shifted with enjoyment in her lawn chair as Ashton started toward us.

Chapter Twelve

I trembled and stared at him.

I knew with Ashton kissing Dixon's ass, that Ashton would be turned on and boy was he ever. His erection was serpent-like, angling upward toward his belly. His cock was flushed red with arousal, and it bounced stiffly with his every step. His dark eyes smoldered with heat.

Behind Ashton, Dixon and Leo separated.

"Your turn," Jenny whispered with a giggle.

Something inside of me went all primal awareness as Dixon and Leo flanked Ashton and all three men now stalked toward me with sexual intent.

My body was humming with exquisite longing as Dixon, Ashton and Leo stopped in front of me.

"We are not boys, our Queen." Dixon growled as he stared me down with those brilliant blue eyes.

His thick voice dripped with lust while the other two prison guards gazed at me with narrow eyed intent. I swallowed at my suddenly dry throat, realizing my teasing of calling them *boys* may have been insulting to them.

"My apologies," I said in a breathless voice.

I sure did not want them mad at me. Not when I was this close to getting what I wanted from them.

Dixon grunted his appreciation and then held out his hand to me.

"Get up off your throne, my queen. We men wish to show you exactly how grown up we are."

Beside me, I heard Jenny moan. It appeared she was enjoying herself.

However, I dared not break the mesmerizing gaze from Dixon as he made me feel as if I was burning alive. I could feel the aching demand for sex throbbing between my thighs and my breasts felt unbearably heavy.

I placed my hand into Dixon's, and he easily hoisted me onto my feet.

Mercy, but he was a strong man.

"Come, move away a bit so we can give Jenny a nice show," he said.

The hypnotic eye contact was broken as he led me about ten feet away from Jenny, who, as I now dared to take a peek at her, sat wide eyed with anticipation. Her legs were spread open to us while her hands were clenched on the lawn chair armrests as she watched us with wide-eyed wonder.

I noticed that Ashton had disappeared behind some nearby trees. A few seconds later, he reappeared with a couple of boxes of condoms and a tube of lubricant in his hands.

My heart was hammering at an insane speed as Leo retrieved the thick red fleece blanket, the one I'd just been sitting on, and he placed it like a red carpet in front of us.

"Off with your shoes and socks, then stand upon your bed, Queen," Dixon instructed.

My legs felt wobbly as I did what he said. When I stepped onto the blanket, it pushed warmth upon the soles of my feet.

From beside me the slurp of lube shot through the air, and I looked over to see that Ashton had already donned a condom and he was generously smearing the lube up and down the heavy-looking length of his very erect shaft.

"Queen, you will love what we're about to give you. But not before Leo and I get our nourishment first," Dixon muttered.

I inhaled sharply as Leo and Dixon stepped closer to me. I could feel the hard press of their bodies against my swollen belly and their cocks branding along the sides of my thighs as the two men palmed my breasts with their warm hands.

Then their heads lowered.

Hot mouths circled my nipples like two scorching brands. I moaned as rough, male lips began pulling and sucking at my throbbing peaks. I cried out as a hand slipped between my thighs, urging me to open my legs.

So, I opened them wide.

I could barely keep my eyes open as I looked down and watched two men suckle milk from my breasts, their luscious lips moving rhythmically.

Then I bucked as a lubed cockhead pressed against my tight sphincter. Warm hands settled upon my waist.

"Just relax," Ashton encouraged from behind me.

I tried, surely, I did.

But the incredible stimulation of two men practically devouring my tender nipples was creating quite a bit of tension between my thighs. My vaginal muscles were spasming with awareness, my clitoris felt hot and engorged, and my ass was clenching with a fierce need to be penetrated.

Suddenly I just wanted to scream at the agony of knowing what was about to happen.

"Easy," Ashton whispered, probably sensing my distress.

His strong hands held tight, and I fought for breath as his cockhead pushed into me. The pressure was so intense, I was panting.

"She's nice and tight," he growled with appreciation.

In response, Dixon and Leo's hands began to intimately pump my breasts. Their warm palms gently squeezed my mounds as they slurped and sucked on my rigid nipples.

I moaned as Ashton's shaft plunged deeper, creating a red-hot pressure that had me keening.

My legs weakened as the two men continued to milk me for nourishment, making my nipples grow harder and incredibly tender. I let out a whimper of pain and the two men eased off but kept suckling, drawing nourishment, and filling their bellies.

Ashton began a slow withdrawal of his cock out of my ass. I could feel every thick inch of his flesh as it teasingly pressured my anal muscles.

Had my breasts not been attached to two greedily sucking mouths and had there not been strong hands holding me steady, I surely would have dropped to the ground as Ashton withdrew.

Then he drove his cock into my ass again, pushing me against Dixon and Leo's hard muscular bodies.

Dixon pressed his bulging cockhead about an inch into my mouth, his hot flesh vibrating against my lips. I gazed over at him, mesmerized once again by those brilliant blue eyes and by the wicked need flaring in his expression.

"Suck it, my Queen," he ordered in a strangled voice.

So, I did.

I tightened my mouth around his pulsing penis, loving the tortured moans escaping from somewhere deep within his chest.

I drew on his flesh, enjoying the raspy sounds of his heavy breaths and in the way his eyes squeezed tight with appreciation.

Then I began licking and dabbing my tongue against his slit, tasting his precum.

I sucked his cockhead some more and soon he was pushing his penis deeper into my mouth.

Unclenching my hands from the blankets, I reached over and pushed his hand away so I could hold the base of his shaft. Then I moved my head forward, allowing as much cock into my mouth as I could. When he touched the back of my throat, I pulled back an inch and then wrapped my other hand around his shaft near my lips to prevent him from jabbing into my throat when he lost control during his orgasm.

I nodded, giving him the okay, and then he slowly began to thrust in and out. I kept my lips constricted, and lapped beneath his shaft with my tongue, enjoying his tortured moans.

Between my thighs, Leo had backed off, allowing Dixon and I to prepare for oral. When he saw Dixon enjoying himself, Leo was right back at it.

He circled my clit with that delightfully big smooth as silk cockhead, creating shivers of excitement rushing through me before he then dipped a couple of inches into my wet vagina and then out.

Deeper and deeper, every time he came into my vagina and then he'd return to pleasuring my clit until every inch of me was burning alive and I was perspiring.

Before long I was writhing upon a moaning Ashton, his cock throbbing and spasming inside my anal channel with my every move.

Flames of pleasure wrapped around me as Leo slowly pistoned his pleasure stick in and out. The pressure of three cocks, one which was quite huge, pulsed inside of me so intensely that I swear I had never felt something so incredible before.

Heat and spasms built quickly and soon I felt as if I'd had been dipped into an inferno of need. Hungrily, I sucked on Dixon's pulsing penis as the tension continued to build within me.

Leo began pistoning faster and faster.

Wicked shudders came out of nowhere and crashed into me.

I suddenly lost it.

I began convulsing, delving deep into the gratifying waves that were so magnificent I couldn't stop myself from mindlessly screaming as I was pummeled by cocks, pleasure, and spasms.

My orgasm went on forever.

It was so beautiful. Better than I had ever imagined it would be. The pleasure of three cocks plunging in and out of me, burned me alive. Flames licked every inch of my body as I writhed and bucked.

Each pleasure spasm was stronger than the last.

The cocks were like steel rods as they impaled me, unleashing rapturous pleasure that exploded through my mind and seared electrical jolts into my every nerve and fibre.

They kept me within the naughty vortex for what seemed like an eternity.

The cocks pistoned harder, faster, and I drowned within a dark kaleidoscope of colors and sensations, which led me into a second climax that was stronger than the first.

And they just kept fucking me.

Fierce, harsh thrusts that had my pussy pulsing and my ass clenched so tight I felt as if my entire body would shatter.

Before long, I slipped into a third orgasm.

It raced through me with lightning speed.

Tremors, upon spasms, upon pleasure. So intense. So wonderful.

Finally, after the last orgasm began to ebb, I just collapsed upon Ashton and felt each of the men finally allowing themselves their release.

I was panting up a storm when their warm hands began gentling my body, caressing my swollen belly, and calming my quivering legs. When I was finally still enough, Dixon and Leo said nothing as they helped me off Ashton. They braced me until I got a firm bearing on my feet.

Then I glanced over to grab Jenny's gaze, craving to see the expression on her pretty face and I was stunned to find her lawn chair empty!

Perhaps she'd slipped away to go to the bathroom?

"She's taken all our clothes," Leo suddenly growled as he let go of me.

She took their clothes, I thought numbly.

I heard an absurd stream of loud curses as the three prison guards began to rush about the area where they'd dropped their clothing and weapons.

"She's taken our weapons and radio too! The van keys were in my shirt pocket!" Dixon shouted.

"Then she's got my van keys too!" Leo spat.

"That bitch!" Ashton cursed as he rushed into the nearby trees. No doubt to check on the prison vehicles. Moments later, he came back with an intense frown.

His eyes were furious, and I just knew then that Jenny had duped us and escaped.

"One of the vans is gone!" Ashton shouted.

Shock and despair rumbled through me.

How could Jenny do this? How could she betray me like this? How could she just take off when she'd just asked me earlier to take her when I broke out of prison again?

Damn! She'd been playing me!

"If you had anything to do with this, Mad, you will be in solitary for the rest of your life," Dixon said with a demonic look.

His furious stare didn't scare me though. There was no proof of me helping Jenny.

I was innocent. I had nothing to fear.

"Sorry to disappoint, boys, but it looks like she planned this all on her own," I confessed.

There was no way I was going down for something Jenny did, especially after she'd played me the way she had.

Man, I felt like I'd just been dumped into one hell of a weird dream.

But a moment later, an inner part of me smiled.

The prison guards had been caught literally with their pants down, while a prisoner had escaped. Again.

Good for you, Jenny!

Chapter Thirteen

My heart was pounding at an insane rate as the unfamiliar guard stopped me in front of a door that said Consultation Room. I had never been in this section of the prison before, especially because of the Authorized Personnel Only signs hanging pretty much everywhere on the walls.

For the last week, since Jenny had escaped, I'd been kept in solitary. Prison guards had dragged me from my cell in wrist and ankle restraints for questioning every day. I'd also been allowed an hour outside in the exercise yard cage.

I had not seen Dixon, Leo, or Ashton since after we'd all been picked up by a prison van after Jenny had escaped.

But the guards had warned me to keep my mouth shut or I would suffer the consequences. So, during my daily questioning sessions, I'd said what the three guards had told me to say right after Jenny had escaped and before we'd been picked up.

I'd been told to say that Jenny had somehow gotten a weapon, held it on us, forced us all to undress and she taken the van with all our clothing and their weapons.

So, when they requested me to leave solitary again today, I figured there were just more questions. But this time things felt different because, as I said, I had never been in this part of the prison before.

The guard who'd led me here, knocked on the door. From the other side I heard a man's voice call out for us to enter. The guard opened the door and nodded for me to go in.

Every instinct in me was yelling at me to make a run for it.

I sensed trouble. Big trouble. But where could I run?

So, I steadied my nerves and entered the room. The door closed behind me with a bang that made me jump.

I whirled around. The guard was gone!

I turned again and discovered a man and a woman seated at a shiny metal table in the far corner. The two looked to me like some kind of officials. They wore very plain clothes. Boring colors of navy blue and black.

My heart began to pound and not in a good way.

I smelled cops.

I'd never seen the woman before but when I focused on the man, I recognized him as that creepy prison guard who'd eyed me so suspiciously those mornings while Leo had put Jenny and I into restraints before heading out to the van.

Which made me wonder. What the fuck was going on?

"Madeline Madison?" the female asked.

"Who wants to know?" I tried to act tough, but my insides were trembling.

I was kind of scared.

"Please take a seat so we can talk."

She didn't give me her name. Instead, she nodded to the lone chair on my side of the table.

I hesitated for a moment and tried to figure out what to do and realized there really wasn't anything I could do except do what she said.

My wrists and ankle chains rattled ominously as I walked over to the table and pulled the chair far out. I needed lots of room for me and the kid, who had been kicking up a storm the last couple of days. I placed my hand upon my belly and caressed the bump, hoping to calm the kid down.

I knew the kid and I would be separated at some point, so I had made sure not to open my heart to it. It was bloody hard though to be emotionless where my unborn baby was concerned.

I sat down and tossed the two officials a fake smile. I waited to see what they wanted.

"Madeline, we'll get straight to the point," the man said.

His gaze was as piercing and unnerving as ever.

Now I knew why.

My instincts told me that he *had* to be a cop. But how was that possible? He was a prison guard.

"Please do get straight to the point. Because you are wasting my time," I stated in a bored tone.

The faster I got out of here, the better.

"Madeline, it's come to our attention that the male guards are taking sexual advantage of the incarcerated women in this prison, you being one of them," the female said.

Her stare burned right through me, and I could feel my face heating up with embarrassment.

Oh, great, my worst nightmare was unfolding right in front of me.

No more sex. No more chain gang. No more Queen. No more power over the guards.

I remained silent. These two would get nothing out of me.

"We've got a proposition for you. We are offering you a full pardon plus full immunity from any prosecution, if you agree to testify against the officers you know as Leo, Dixon, and Ashton."

I felt my mouth drop open in shock.

Man, a full freaking pardon?

I could get out of here. I could stay with my baby.

But another idea entered my mind.

Was this some elaborate scheme that the guards had manufactured to see if I would cave under pressure? Yeah, it had to be a test to see if I would break.

"I'm sorry. I have no idea what you're talking about," I said firmly.

The female didn't smile. She just nodded. Then she turned to a full-length wardrobe style mirror on a nearby wall and waved.

Oh man. Was I being watched? It had to be a two-way mirror. Dixon, Leo, and Ashton had to be on the other side checking to see if I would talk.

Suddenly a door beside the mirror, swung open.

Jenny walked in.

Oh man!

Had Jenny been caught already?

I tried to catch her gaze.

Tried to warn her to keep her mouth shut with a cautionary look, but she confidently walked in and came to stand behind the other two seated people.

She smiled that pretty smile that made me feel happy inside.

"Hi, Mad. I'm Detective Jennifer Walton of the Vice Squad. I've been undercover here."

She held out a badge. I stared at it in stunned disbelief.

I gazed up at her, realizing she wasn't wearing any prison clothing. Instead, she wore a boring navy-blue pantsuit. Her baby bump seemed smaller.

Instinctively, I knew she'd had her baby.

"Holy shit," I murmured as the shock disintegrated and reality finally hit.

Jenny was a freaking police officer. An undercover cop.

Suddenly, I felt like I couldn't breathe. It was a good thing I was sitting down because I kind of felt faint.

"Are you okay?" Jenny asked in a soft voice that gave me the feeling she truly cared about me.

"Would you be? I thought you abandoned me," I gasped.

Wow, that sounded lame. I'd only known her for a couple of days, and I already cared for her like she was a dear friend.

"I'm sorry, I had to deceive you in the way that I did. I lied about an abusive husband and losing my babies. It was my cover story when we infiltrated the prison. We need to take these guards down. I finally got all the information I needed to give to the authorities to get the ball rolling. One of those prison guards is the father of your baby. He most likely will go to prison if you and a few other inmates agree to testify against him and the others. With my testimony and yours and if I can get other inmates to talk, you can be rid of any claim Dixon has on your child."

Now that would be an interesting thing to happen. To get rid of Dixon and any rights he had on my baby would be ideal.

Not that I didn't like the sex I'd experienced with all three of my prison guards, because I certainly had enjoyed the menages. But making me pregnant, on purpose, without my consent, was just not good daddy material, in my opinion.

Besides, I had to look out for myself and for my kid. I would be stupid not to take the deal. And, sex, I could get anywhere, especially if I were free of prison.

My mind began whirling with possibilities of how I could maximize this opportunity.

My testimony would be a gold mine, and I figured I should get more than a pardon.

"What is this immunity from prosecution that you mentioned? I didn't do anything wrong." Except have consensual sex with the prison guards.

"In case the prison guards accuse you of something inappropriate, you would get immunity as part of the deal to testify," Jenny replied.

"Seriously? Like you would have that kind of leverage?" I asked.

"Yes, a judge has already agreed to sign off on all of it, if you agree to testify."

This was nuts. But in a really cool way.

"How many prison guards are going down?" I asked.

"Well, I am not at liberty to say, but it stretches out to be more than the three you were involved with. Had we not been tipped off that something was going on here, you would most likely have been handed over to many other prison guards with different fetishes."

Wow, really. So, this prison guard fetish thing with the female inmates was bigger than Dixon, Ashton, and Leo.

"I've got conditions," I spat out, feeling the power shift through me like a mighty warrior.

"Okay," Jenny replied with a wink. "Tell us what you want and let's see if we can get it for you."

"Man, I knew I liked you for a reason," I complimented her.

Hey, kissing people's asses certainly worked for me over the course of my life, and I was pretty sure it would work in this case too.

TWENTY-FOUR HOURS LATER I was out of my irritating wrist and ankle restraints, out of prison forever and having my baby in a hospital, instead of the prison infirmary.

Jenny was the only one who I told I was in labor, mainly because my contractions had begun the instant the authorities had agreed to my terms, and she'd stayed with me the entire labor. We'd talked a lot between my contractions.

She told me she'd felt her contractions beginning that same day I'd been triple penetrated. The guards had been so pre-occupied in pleasuring me, she'd had no problem gathering up their clothing and their weapons and taking off in the van.

She'd driven straight to the hospital where she'd had a baby boy and named him Sean Douglas. She'd also let me know she was married to that creepy guard I hadn't liked, who'd also been a plant to keep an eye on Jenny making sure she was safe.

She'd been a little over a month pregnant when her boss had asked her and her husband if they'd wanted this gig of exposing the guards. They'd agreed.

She told me she and her husband, Jackson, lived for these adrenalin-rush daring undercover assignments. They got off on helping people and catching the bad guys. She also confessed that her husband and herself had an open marriage and she could see anyone she wanted.

I liked that last part of her being able to see anyone she wanted. Even though she had deceived me, I was glad she'd had her baby, and that she was safe.

"It's a girl. A healthy baby girl," the female doctor announced with a warm smile from between my legs.

Oh, sweet mercy! I had a baby girl! How cool was that?

My daughter began to cry, and I had an overwhelming urge to comfort her.

"I need to see her," I whispered.

My pain of giving birth was completely forgotten as my heart clenched with intense love for my unseen baby.

"The nurse will clean her up for you. It'll just be a few minutes," the doctor reassured me with a huge smile.

Jenny smiled too, and grabbed my hand, squeezing my fingers.

"Congratulations!" she said.

"I'm a mother," I whispered as a few very impatient moments later, I eagerly accepted my little baby bundle.

"Wow are you ever cute," I said to my baby.

She had the cutest upturned nose. My nose, which I had always liked.

"She has your cupid shaped lips and your sweet nose," Jenny pointed out.

She did not mention my baby's hair color or the color of her eyes. Dixon's hair and Dixon's eyes.

But that didn't matter one bit because my little baby's eyes were smiling at me.

My heart clenched.

She loves me.

"I love you so much," I whispered and hugged her.

"There is a guard outside your door for your protection and once they discharge you, the three of us will head back to the safe house where you'll meet my baby," Jenny stated.

I nodded and exhaled a huge sigh of relief. I couldn't wait to meet her son.

My daughter and I would be okay too. Jenny had agreed to be one of my bodyguards during my stay at the safe house. That had been one of my conditions and I was glad she had agreed.

During the trials, they would be keeping me at a top-secret place. I'd even negotiated a generous monthly income so I could take care of myself and my baby's needs for as long as they needed me to testify.

After the trials, we would be flown to Greece. I had always wanted to go there.

Jenny said she knew a couple of guys who lived there, and they were already on the lookout for a small house to rent on one of the Greek islands for me and my baby.

Then I would get a job and then my baby girl, and I could move on with life.

"Have you got a name for her yet?" Jenny asked.

I stared at my daughter long and hard until a beautiful name popped into my mind.

"Elizabeth Rose," I answered.

"It's perfect," Jenny whispered.

"Yes, it is," I nodded and hugged my daughter tighter.

I had never felt happier in my life as I did right now.

The End

Spunky Girl Publishing Catalog

Jasmine Black ~Erotica

(a.k.a. Jan Springer writing as Jasmine Black)
Here are some Jasmine Black stories.

Taken by Two Prison Guards

TWENTY-THREE-YEAR-OLD Madeline "Mad" Madison has quite the temper. She got ten to life in prison due to her getting mad at her late boyfriend and there's only one naughty way she knows of to keep herself calm and she's not getting *that* type of rehabilitation in prison. That is, until she's assigned hard labor on a chain gang and is taken by two prison guards.

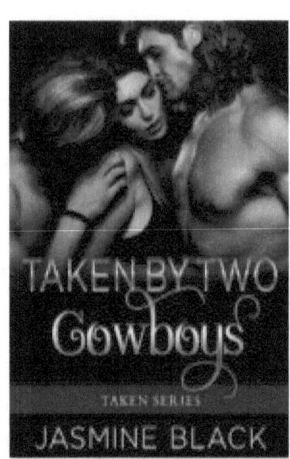

Taken by Two Cowboys

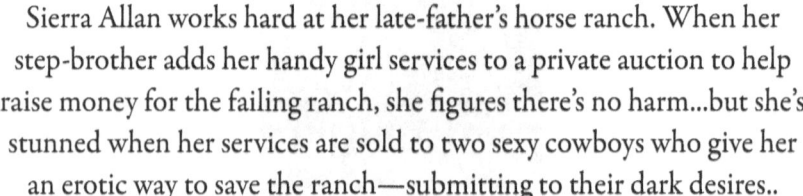

Sierra Allan works hard at her late-father's horse ranch. When her step-brother adds her handy girl services to a private auction to help raise money for the failing ranch, she figures there's no harm...but she's stunned when her services are sold to two sexy cowboys who give her an erotic way to save the ranch—submitting to their dark desires..

Taken by Three Billionaires

Billionaire friends, Liam, Theo and Elijah have just won Princess Isabella in a billionaire card game. Isabella knows exactly what the three men will want from her...she just hadn't expected to have all three of them at once!

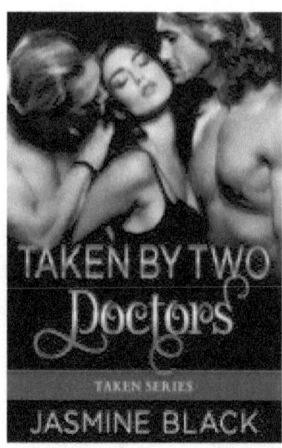

Taken by Two Doctors
A BDSM Medical Fetish Erotica Quickie MFM

Waitress Jean Spelling visits her controversial doctor once a month for some much-needed...stress relief. She looks forward to putting her feet up in the stirrups and enjoys Dr. Ball's naughty unconventional treatments. This time when she arrives, she's surprised to discover that she'll be physically examined by two doctors and they'll prescribe her some much-needed release right there on the examination table!

Ménage series
Taken by Three Bodyguards
Taken by Three Bikers
Taken by Three Billionaires
Taken by Three Doctors
Taken by Three Cowboys
Taken by Three Prison Guards

Taken series.
Taken by Two X-Husbands
Taken by Two Sugar Daddies
Taken by Two Prison Guards
Taken by Two Elves
Taken by Two Mountain Men
Taken by Two Cops
Taken by Two Santas
Taken by Two Lifeguards
Taken by Two Firefighters
Taken by Two Bikers
Taken by Two Billionaires
Taken by Two Bosses
Taken by Two Cowboys
Taken by Two Personal Trainers
Taken by Two Carpenters

Jasmine Black Website ~ http://www.jasmine-black.com
Twitter ~ @blackerotica1

Jan Springer ~ Erotic Romance ~

Cowboys For Christmas
Cowboys Online 1 ~ Moose Ranch #1
Jan Springer
A Canadian Contemporary Ménage Romance m/f/m/m Series

Jennifer Jane (JJ) Watson has spent the past ten Christmases in a maximum-security prison.

The last thing she expects is to get early parole, along with a job on a remote Canadian cattle ranch serving Christmas holiday dinners to three of the sexiest cowboys she's ever met!

Rafe, Brady and Dan thought they were getting a couple of male ex-cons to help out around their secluded ranch, but instead they get an attractive and very appealing female.

In the snowbound wilds of Northern Ontario, female companionship is rare.

It's a good thing the three men like to share...

They're dominating, sexy-as-sin and they fill JJ with the hottest ménage fantasies she's ever had. Suddenly she's craving cowboys for Christmas and wishing for something she knows she can never have...a happily ever after.

Cowboys In Her Pocket
Cowboys Online 2 ~ Moose Ranch #2
Jan Springer

After spending ten years in a maximum-security prison Jennifer Jane (JJ) Watson got early parole and a job on a remote Canadian cattle ranch playing housekeeper to three of the sexiest cowboys she's ever met...

Spring has finally arrived at Moose Ranch, and a single woman fresh out of prison shouldn't be experiencing scorching ménages with her three sexy-as-sin cowboys. But JJ's love for her men continues to grow as she gives into the fevered heat and scorching passions she feels for each of them.

Life is perfect.

Until her new life is tested when mysterious happenings occur on the ranch and then one of her cowboys is viciously attacked and injured.

Will JJ's newfound freedom and happiness be ripped away?

Rafe, Brady and Dan never expected to find an attractive and very appealing female to help them out at their secluded ranch. But in the wilds of Northern Ontario, female companionship is rare. It's a good thing the three men like to share...

Brady, Dan and Rafe have never been happier. Their cattle ranch is flourishing and their continued desire to share the sexy woman who cares for them makes their life complete. Until danger threatens to rip everything apart...

Loving Her Cowboys
Cowboys Online 3 ~ Moose Ranch #3
Jan Springer

AFTER SPENDING TEN years in a maximum-security prison Jennifer Jane (JJ) Watson got early parole and a job on a remote Canadian cattle ranch playing housekeeper to three of the sexiest cowboys she's ever met...

Her love for her cowboys continues to grow as she gives into fevered heat. But JJ's simmering restlessness explodes and she's seriously making up for lost time by pursuing her dreams. There's only one little problem. She hasn't revealed to her bosses what she's been up to while they're away tending to the cattle. She knows when they discover her secret, there will be hell to pay.

Ranchers Rafe, Dan and Brady have found the woman who completes them. She makes their secluded ranch a home-sweet-home. She's vulnerable, sweet and willing to share her bed with all three of them. But when JJ's secret is unwittingly revealed, they're stunned and angry. They figure it's time to dole out some fiery punishment in some mighty naughty ways...

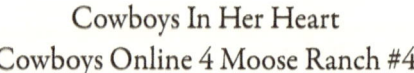

Cowboys In Her Heart
Cowboys Online 4 Moose Ranch #4

AFTER SPENDING TEN years in a maximum-security prison, JJ gets unexpected parole and a job on a Canadian ranch serving up scrumptious dinners and lots of hot love to three of the sexiest cowboys she's ever met.

Jennifer Jane "JJ" Watson has never been happier. She's going to have a baby!

Thankfully their wilderness ranch is a nice distraction for her three sexy cowboys while she's away flying her plane. But when she's home, her dominant hunks are tending to her naughty pregnant cravings and that includes plenty of sizzling ménages.

Rafe, Brady and Dan don't much like the idea of their woman flying the Canadian skies and being at the mercy of the unpredictable

Northern Ontario weather. They would prefer having her warming their beds twenty-four seven. But she has a way of getting what she wants and right now she needs her new-found freedom.

Worst fears are realized when JJ, her friend and JJ's plane suddenly go missing and she doesn't come back home to them.

Always Her Cowboys
Cowboys Online 5 ~ Moose Ranch #5

1

A Canadian Contemporary Ménage Romance m/f/m/m

JENNIFER JANE (JJ) Watson has spent ten Christmases in a maximum-security prison. The last thing she expected was to get early parole, along with a job on a remote Canadian cattle ranch serving Christmas holiday dinners to three of the sexiest cowboys she's ever met!

Rafe, Brady and Dan thought they were getting male ex-cons to help out around their secluded ranch, but instead they got an attractive and very appealing female. In the snowbound wilds of Northern Ontario, female companionship is rare. It's a good thing the three men like to share...

Christmas is coming once again to Moose Ranch and with JJ's due date approaching, she's distracting herself from anxiety attacks by keeping herself ultra-busy preparing for the arrival of her baby and planning Moose Ranch's first annual Christmas party!

1. https://janspringerauthor.files.wordpress.com/2017/11/alwayshercowboys_ebook-1new.jpg

In having a wee baby on the way, there's a lot of stress for Brady, Rafe and Dan. Especially due to JJ's decision on having a wilderness mid-wife deliver the baby *at their secluded ranch* - with *all* of them present for the birth! But their concerns don't stop the men from showing JJ how much they love her...out of bed and in!

With wicked snowstorms, a grounded bush plane, a cheerful holiday party and a sweet baby on the way, the owners of Moose Ranch know this will be one sparkling Christmas season they won't soon forget...

Her Forever Cowboys
Cowboys Online 6 ~ Snowy Creek Ranch #1 (mfmm)
AFTER SPENDING YEARS in prison, Milena Allen is conditionally released and given a job at a secluded Canadian horse ranch where she's instantly attracted to her three sexy cowboy bosses!

When Cowboys Online sends Mitch, Daegen and Paul, a female ex-con to help out around their wilderness ranch, they realize life has been lonely without female companionship. Despite being without women for so long, they vow Milena is off limits.

When violence threatens her cowboys, Milena's nursing skills are put to the test, and she realizes she's falling head over straw hats for her sexy bosses. Soon she discovers all three men are interested in her too! But they keep treating her like one of the guys!

She's always wanted someone to love her and for a place that she can call home. Can Mitch, Daegen and Paul, make her dreams come true? Or will a horrific mistake by Cowboys Online unravel everything?

Claiming Her Cowboys
Cowboys Online 7 Moose Ranch #6

*Jennifer Jane (JJ) Watson spent ten years in a maximum-security prison.
The last thing she expected was to get an early release, along with a job on
a remote Canadian cattle ranch caring for three of the sexiest cowboys
she's ever met!*

*Rafe, Brady and Dan thought they were getting a couple of male ex-cons
to help out around their secluded ranch, but instead they get an attractive
and very appealing female.
In the wilds of Northern Ontario, female companionship is rare so it's a
good thing the three men like to share...*

*They're dominating, sexy-as-sin and they give JJ the hottest ménages
plus one adorable baby!*

But her second pregnancy comes as one giant surprise, and JJ's anxiety overwhelms her when she doesn't know who the father is.

Is it Rafe, Dan or Brady?

Spring days on this ranch are bursting with hard work, danger and emergencies but nights are filled with scorching passions and naughty pleasures as JJ lays claim to her three sexy cowboys.

STORIES IN THE COWBOYS Online Series:

Cowboys for Christmas ~ Book One – Moose Ranch #1 Cowboys Online #1 -Free

Cowboys in Her Pocket ~ Book Two – Moose Ranch #2 Cowboys Online #2

Loving Her Cowboys ~ Book Three – Moose Ranch #3 Cowboys Online #3

Cowboys In Her Heart ~ Book Four – Moose Ranch #4 Cowboys Online #4

Always Her Cowboys ~ Book Five – Moose Ranch #5 Cowboys Online #5

Her Forever Cowboys ~ Book Six – Snowy Creek Ranch #1 Cowboys Online #6

Claiming Her Cowboys ~ Book Seven – Moose Ranch #6 Cowboys Online #7

Risqué Girl Delights Boxed Set
(Contemporary Erotic Romance)

...a touch of romance, a ménage or both?

Edible Delights

YEARS AGO ALLIE MASTERS lost herself in the scorching passion of a ménage a trois relationship with her two bosses. In order to regain her independence, she walked away.

Max and Nick were very fulfilled with their gorgeous assistant. The lovemaking was breathtaking and both men willingly shared the woman they wanted to spend the rest of their lives with. Then she left.

Now Max and Nick have decided it's time to seduce Allie back into their lives.

Toygasm

IT'S A CASE OF MISTAKEN identity when the two owners of Sexy Toys, show up for an erotic several day photo shoot of their toys with famous nude model Cammie Creek.

---

2. https://janspringerauthor.files.wordpress.com/2015/02/rgdelights_box_js_3d_noshadow-1.jpg

Cammie believes the two hunks are the male models she's supposed to work with. Usually she doesn't mix business with pleasure, but when they're seducing her right there in front of the camera, she can't resist turning them into her own personal naughty toys.

Josh and Jode are enjoying the perks of being male models; hot lust, sizzling toys and the best pleasure they've ever had. But how will Cammie react when she discovers they're actually her bosses and not just male models?

Shy Girl

FINALLY FREE OF AN abusive relationship, "Shy Girl" Emma McCall sheds her inhibitions and explores her sensual side at Club Rendezvous, a club specializing in the Alternate Lifestyle.

At the club she's surprised to find Logan Masters, a sexy hunk she's secretly fantasized about since college. With Logan's help, Emma will experience her ultimate fantasy - a scorching ménage a trois.

Roman and Julietta

HER PERFECT LOVER...

Modern day pirate Julietta Black's life has always been immersed in the violent and traditional ways of piracy. When her family's arch enemy puts a hit out on her family, Julietta knows there's only one way to lift the hit; she must kidnap the enemy's sexy grandson and force a union between the two warring families. Night after night, wrapped in Roman's strong arms, she can't deny the searing attraction blazing between them. Nor can she deny he now holds her heart as well as her life in his hands.

His dream angel...

When Roman Prince's mysterious captor offers him a luscious woman to bed, fierce desire ignites, melting his usually tight self-control. Lust quickly turns to love as he enjoys their naughty trysts more than he should. How will he react when he discovers he's been kidnapped, not for a ransom, but captured for his sperm?

Alpha Outlaws Boxed Set (Books 1-5 Outlaw Lovers)
5 Books!!

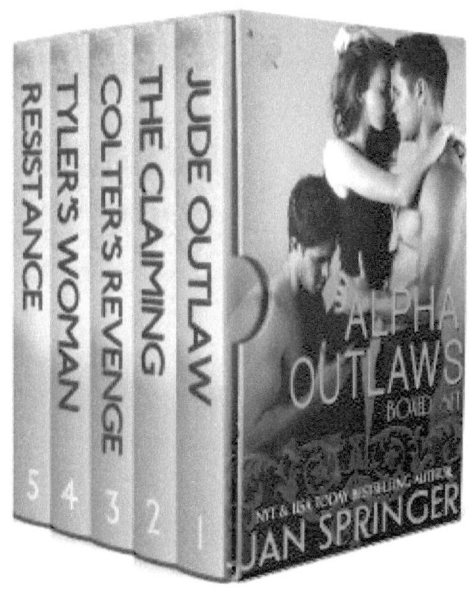

3

IN A WORLD GONE MAD...

A fast-acting virus has killed a majority of the world's female population. With the creation of The Claiming Law, groups of men suddenly have the right to claim a female as their sensual property and the sexy Outlaw brothers are going to declare ownership of the women they love...any way they can.

Jude Outlaw

When Cate Callahan learns Jude is coming home from the Terrorist Wars and is ready to claim her under the new law—with the help of his four brothers—she steals their boat and escapes to the high seas. Unfortunately, her runaway bid for freedom doesn't last long.

Quickly capturing his lover, Jude rekindles the flames and seduces Cate back into his bed.

But Jude holds a secret that could make him lose Cate forever...
PLUS

The Claiming

Seeking refuge from the Claiming Law, Callie Callahan hides in a deserted cabin in the Maine woods and is shocked when her ex-flame finds her. She's always craved being in Luke Outlaw's arms. Tasting him. Touching him. Taking him deeply within her. So, what's a girl to do but to delve into the sinful delights he offers.

Luke has finally reunited with the love of his life. He knows there is only one way to keep Callie safe and with him forever. He'll do it with the help of his three brothers and an assortment of naughty toys. Rekindling the flames between them, he unleashes Callie's sensual side, taking her in ways she never dreamed possible, all with the ultimate goal of introducing her to the Outlaw Lovers and The Claiming.

Colter's Revenge

Revenge belongs to Dr. Colter Outlaw when he unexpectedly reunites with the beautiful woman who broke his heart during the Terrorist Wars. Capturing her, collaring her and holding her against her will, he seduces her, fills her with wicked desires and naughty cravings for a delicious ménage. Fully intent on breaking her heart and walking away, Colter's plans unravel when he submits to the carnal pleasures Ashley gives him so freely.

Colter had told her he loved her. He'd whispered promises of rescue from her life as a slave, but when he'd suddenly disappeared, she'd been devastated. Infected with a version of the X-virus that leaves Ashley Blakely sexually excited on a daily basis, she has come to Pleasure Palace to bid on a cure for her illness. She never expected her Outlaw Lover to be there and screw her plans. Nor did she expect to give him her heart and body so easily...

Tyler's Woman

For years Tyler Outlaw and his best friend, Hunter Brown, endured brutal torture and worse in an overseas terrorist prison. Finally, free of their hell, they return home intent on seducing Laurie into their erotic-filled fantasies.

Laurie Callahan has always experienced red-hot pleasure and passionate love in Tyler Outlaw's arms. But when he's pronounced MIA, presumed dead in the Terrorist Wars, Laurie's world is shattered, and her heart is broken.

Shocked to discover Tyler is alive and he's taken a male lover, Laurie is thrust into a sensual world of sizzling seductions, scorching ménages and the carnal desires that both scarred men crave. But she fears Tyler won't want her when he discovers she's not the same woman he left behind...

****READER CAUTION IS ADVISED (m/m forced scenes) ****

Resistance

In the near future, a virus has been unleashed, killing a majority of the world's female population, forcing the introduction of the Claiming Law. A law that states men have all the rights and women are sexual property claimable by groups of men.

Fugitive female...

Renegade Resistance leader Reena "Red" Wilde is in for the fight of her life when she experiences an erotic attraction to the two most dangerous men she's ever met.

Black ops assassin...

Months ago, Will "Blade" Smith spent one sizzling evening in the arms of a red-haired seductress. Now she's his next assignment. One look into her gorgeous eyes and he's wrestling his heated cravings for her all over again.

Bounty Hunter...

When Cade Outlaw nabs his bounty, sexy-as-sin Reena Wilde, his profession dictates she's hands-off. But he can't ignore the magnetic sparks between them...or that she is the biggest temptation of his life.

Resistance is futile...

After Reena escapes Cade and Will and falls prey to a band of evil hunters, she's grateful her sexy hunks come to her rescue...and in return, saves their lives. Trapped in a solitary cabin during a wicked snowstorm, she can't resist her two, well-hung studs, nor can she deny they've claimed her heart.

Many more Jasmine Black and Jan Springer digital books, print books, audiobooks plus translated digital books and print books can be found at http://www.janspringer.com and http://www.jasmine-black.com

Here are ways we can connect:

Jasmine Black Website at http://janspringerauthor.wordpress.com/jasmine-black/

Jan Springer Website at http://www.janspringer.com[1]

Instagram – http://www.instagram.com/janspringerauthor

Facebook - https://www.facebook.com/janspringereroticromance

Twitter Jan Springer- https://twitter.com/janspringer @janspringer

Twitter Jasmine Black - https://twitter.com/blackerotica1 @blackerotica1

Pinterest - http://www.pinterest.com/janspringer1/

Jan's Blog - http://janspringerauthor.wordpress.com/blog-2/

Happy Reading,

Jasmine Black / Jan Springer

---

1. http://www.janspringer.com/

Don't miss out!

Visit the website below and you can sign up to receive emails whenever Jasmine Black publishes a new book. There's no charge and no obligation.

https://books2read.com/r/B-A-GIJD-ROVQC

Connecting independent readers to independent writers.